Peggy of the C

The Chalet School series by Elinor M. Brent-Dyer

Elinor M. Brent-Dyer

Peggy of the Chalet School

Armada

First published in the U.K. in 1950 by
W. & R. Chambers Ltd, London and Edinburgh
This abridged edition was first published in Armada in 1976 by
Fontana Paperbacks,
8 Grafton Street, London W1X 3LA

Armada is an imprint of Fontana Paperbacks,
part of the Collins Publishing Group

This impression 1987

© Copyright reserved

Printed in Great Britain by
William Collins Sons & Co. Ltd, Glasgow

Chapter One

ENTER PEGGY!

The Lady Acetylene Lampe reclined at ease on the broad window-seat, and gazed dreamily out over the sea which lay hot, sparkling, and brilliantly blue on this August morning.

"My lady," said her faithful attendant, "whither are thy thoughts straying? With thy lord, perchance, who even now does battle for his king and country in the vasty fields of France? Or——"

"Peace, wench!" the Lady Acetylene interrupted peevishly. "You disturb the—the parabola of my mind."

The faithful attendant gasped. "The — *what* of your mind?" she asked feebly.

"You heard!" her Lady retorted briefly.

"Where did you get it?" the faithful attendant demanded. Then she added with point, "D'you know what it *means*? Come to that, can you even *spell* it?"

Before the outraged Lady Acetylene could reply, there came a further interruption. A plaintive voice called up the stairs, "Polly—*Pol-lee*! Come down, dear! I want you!"

"There's Mother on the yell," the attendant observed, with a most undutiful lack of respect. "What does she want now?"

"You'd better go and see," the Lady responded. "It can't be to lay the table for tea. I did that before we came up here."

"*My* name's not Polly. It's you she's yelling for."

"Well, you can go and find out, can't you?"

"I don't see why I should have to run all your errands,"

the faithful attendant grumbled, nevertheless rising from her three-legged stool, and going to the door.

"Of course you can. It's good for little girls to fag for their elder sisters," the Lady replied sweetly.

For answer, the faithful attendant plumped herself down on the nearest chair and glared defiantly at her mistress. "You can jolly well go yourself for that!"

"Polly—*Pollee!*" The cry came up the stairs again.

"Oh, bother and bust it!" The Lady sat up with due care for the three cushions, two pillows, and rolled-up eiderdown against which she had been reclining. "Go on, Lala, there's a good kid! I'm all tied up with this beastly curtain, and if one of us doesn't go there'll be a row if Father hears of it when he comes home. You know what he said last week, and he's due to-morrow, so there's no chance of Mother forgetting if he asks for details."

The faithful attendant got slowly to her feet. "It's only 'cos I don't want another row like last week's," she warned the Lady, as she turned once more to the door. Then she stopped short, her ear caught by the sound of light feet running up the stairs. "I say! Who's this coming?" she hissed in a half whisper to the Lady, who had lain back against her cushionings again. " 'Tisn't Mother, anyhow!"

Before the Lady could either reply or move, there came a tap at the door, and Lala moved automatically to open it. On the threshold stood a slight, fair girl who was looking rather shy at the moment, though her blue eyes widened as she caught sight of the recumbent figure draped in an old damask curtain, and sprawling on the window-seat below the wide dormer window.

"Hello!" Lala greeted the newcomer rather doubtfully, while her sister, once more sitting up, this time with a jerk that sent the pillows and a cushion to the floor, stared with dropping jaw. "I say, aren't you one of the Bettany girls who live at the Quadrant?"

"Yes, I'm Peggy Bettany, the eldest," the stranger replied, as she came forward into the untidy room.

"Well, come on and sit down," Lala invited her.

6

Peggy went up to the only unoccupied seat, an aged wicker chair, but was stopped by a cry from Lala.

"Hi! Don't sit on that! 'Tisn't safe! Here; try this!" and she hastily tossed a couple of sandy towels off a carved spinning chair and set it for their guest.

Peggy sat down, and turned to look at the somewhat abashed Lady, who was trying to disentangle herself from her coverings and couch.

"Your mother met mine at Mrs. Anstey's yesterday afternoon," she said explanatorily, "and she told her how hard she found it to get any help. Our housemaid, Loveday, has a cousin who's a widow, and she wants work. Mummy thought if Mrs. Pender hadn't found a job, she might do for you. She asked Loveday when she came home, and Mrs. Pender would love to come here because it's fairly close at hand for her. She lives in one of those cottages round the bend in the road." Here Peggy pointed to the road which she could see through the window if she stood up. "Mummy came up to tell Mrs. Winterton about her, and I came with her as there were some parcels to take to the post first. Mrs. Winterton called to you, but you didn't hear, so I offered to come up and find you."

By the time this lengthy speech was ended, the Lady had contrived to dispose of her coverings and was standing up. Peggy glanced at her. She saw a tall, lanky girl, a good head taller than herself, with a wavy shock of very dark red hair that would have been the better for a good brushing and combing, a fresh, pink and white skin liberally befreckled, and heavily-lashed hazel eyes, at present rather sulky. She wore a frock of butcher-blue cotton that had seen better days, and her long bare legs were sunburnt and scratched.

"We're Polly and Lala," this person said brusquely. "I'm Polly, this is Lala—Mary and Alice, really."

Peggy laughed. "Isn't it awful the way you're given one name, and called another?" she said easily. "I'm Margaret, of course, but no one ever calls me anything but Peggy or Peg. My twin brother is Richard, and always Rix. Fearfull" She changed the subject. "How do you like Chan-

7

ning St. Mary? You've been here six weeks now, haven't you?"

"Oh, it's not too dusty," Polly said, stooping to pick up the pillows, which she tossed on to the nearest bed, following them with the cushion and her curtain. "I say," as she stood up again, "it's hottish up here. You take Peggy down to the garden, Lal, and I'll come in a minute. I must make myself decent first."

She had moved so that she was behind Peggy, and now she gave her sister a signal which that young woman knew meant, "Do as I ask and don't ask questions!" Being an easy-tempered young person on the whole, Lala winked the eye that Peggy couldn't see, and said heartily, "Good scheme! Come on, Peggy! We'll go and park under the walnut, and Polly'll be down in a sec."

The two left the room together, and once they were gone, Polly set to work to make a lightning change. She had felt a regular grub beside dainty Peggy! Off came her frock, a clean one appeared from the closet, and she wriggled into it at full speed. She kicked off the dirty tennis shoes she had worn, and found her sandals, which were several degrees better. Then she caught up Lala's hairbrush which was lying on the dressing-table, and battered her head with it ferociously, reducing her hair to a semblance of tidiness, though it lacked the soft sheen of the fair curls peeping under Peggy's big hat. She hunted out a length of black ribbon velvet with which she banded her recalcitrant locks, and then made for the bathroom, where she washed her face and hands with a will. After a final glance at herself as she passed the hall mirror, she followed the other two out into the big, untidy garden, looking considerably better for her hurried toilet.

Lala opened saucer-like eyes when her sister joined them under the aged walnut tree at the bottom of the garden, and she opened her lips to say something; but Polly gave her a look so fierce and threatening, that she closed them again without speaking. Peggy moved up the rickety garden seat to make room, and Polly had to sit down before her sister could think of anything to say.

8

"I love a walnut tree to sit under in summer," the visitor remarked. "It's about the only tree I know where you're reasonably safe from flies."

"It's fairly cool, anyhow," Polly said in her funny, abrupt way. "Lala, you do look a mess! Scoot in and change, for pity's sake!"

Lala looked prepared to argue this; but again Polly quenched her with a look, and she got up meekly and departed to make herself more fit to be seen, while her sister and Peggy Bettany surveyed each other thoughtfully, and tried to think of something to say. Peggy succeeded first.

"I think Mrs. Winterton told Mummy that you lived in Yorkshire before you came here?" she said. "This must be a good deal of a change for you. How do you like it?"

"Oh, it's all right," the hostess replied. "It's got the sea and a decent shore, anyway. Where we lived before, we were miles inland."

"Where was that?" Peggy asked with interest. "Was it anywhere near Garnton-on-the-moors? We have a family house there. I mean, all the family shares it, and takes it in turn to go there for hols. Did you live anywhere near?"

Polly shook her head. "No; we lived up in the Pennines —on the moors, though. We could see the Peak from our top windows on clear days. I've heard of Garnton, of course, but I've never been there. We used to go to North Wales when we went anywhere—though, come to that, we didn't often go there, either. Granpa is the vicar at Pwllylleyn, a tiny town in Carnarvonshire, about five miles from the sea."

"We've never been in North Wales," Peggy said thoughtfully.

"Are you going to Garnton this summer?" Polly asked.

"No; some of the aunts have it, and we were there at Easter. They have six kids among them, and Wolferl and Josefa were having friends to stay as well, so there wasn't any room. It isn't much more than a big cottage. There are six of us, you know, as well as Mummy and Daddy."

9

"You've two little kids, I know. I've seen them with Mrs. Bettany," Polly said.

"Yes; Second Twins—Maurice and Maeve."

"Second Twins? Why on earth d'you call them that?"

"Because they *are*. Rix and I are twins, and the eldest. Then comes Bride, who is a year younger—just fifteen. Jackie is next; he's thirteen. And then Second Twins, who are ten."

"Do you mean to say you're sixteen?" Polly asked incredulously.

Peggy nodded. "Sixteen last January, worse luck! So I've only this year and next at school. Then I'm coming home. Mummy needs me. She's awfully lonely in term-time when we're all away, and then we have sheep and cattle and poultry, and there are all the gardens as well. It'll be fun, but I shall miss school horribly at first, I expect."

Polly was not paying attention to this. "Good *night*!" she ejaculated. Then she began to laugh. "I thought you were only about fourteen—the same age as Lala. *What* did you say your next sister is called? *Bride*? What a weird name! I've never heard it before."

"Oh, yes, you have," Peggy told her serenely. "What about St. Bride's Bay? Bride is short for Bridget which is her proper name. I told you people are given names and then called something else. The kids are the only ones that get their full baptismal names in our house. But I don't see," she added thoughtfully, "just what you *could* use as short for Maurice and Maeve."

"There was a boy living near us in Yorkshire who was Maurice, and his folk called him Mossy," Polly suggested.

"How ghastly! I say, don't let young Maeve hear that. She's a demon, and she'd freeze on to it at once, and then there'd be fireworks from Maurice. He's a sweet-tempered kid as a rule, but he wouldn't put up with that, and I shouldn't blame him, either!" Once more, Peggy changed the subject. "You have brothers, too, haven't you?"

"Only one of our own. The eldest is a step," Polly told her. "When Father wasn't much more than a kid, he married, and Giles is their child. She died of bronchitis

10

when Giles was about three, and a few years later he met Mother and married her, and there were us three—me, Lala, and Freddy. I'm fifteen—my birthday is in January too—and Lala will be fourteen at the end of next month. Freddy's away with Father; they're coming home to-morrow. He'll be eleven at the end of December, poor kid! It's tough luck having your birthday so near Christmas. Folks give you birthday and Christmas presents in one."

Peggy nodded. "I know. We're January 30th, so we just escape that. Your Freddy is just the right age for our kids. There aren't any round here. It doesn't matter during the term, of course. We're all away at school. Rix is at Winchester, and Jackie at Dartmouth, and Maurice at a prep near Winchester; and we girls go to the Chalet School. Term time's all right. But in the hols Second Twins have only each other. They'll be thrilled to hear of another boy of their own age so near at hand."

Polly stared at her. "Freddy doesn't play much with girls," she remarked in her abrupt way.

"He'll have to take Maeve on if he wants Maurice," their sister retorted. "The kids share everything. We had awful scenes when they were parted for school. They've got over that, of course; but in the hols, they're rarely apart. You'll find he won't mind. Maeve is more like a boy than a girl. She can climb anything climbable; her whistle is enough to deafen one; she's got a really straight eye—she's a demon with a cricket ball; dead on the wicket, every time!—she can run like a hare, and she doesn't seem to know what fear is. I don't think your Freddy will worry much about her being a *girl*—especially as she nearly lives in shorts and shirts this weather."

"Oh?" was all Polly could think of in reply to this.

Lala appeared at this juncture, looking considerably better for a wash and brush-up and a clean frock. She was quite unlike Polly in appearance, being small and daintily made, with straight brown hair which she wore parted in the centre, and brushed smoothly down either side of her small, three-cornered face. Unlike Polly, who freckled or burned but never tanned, she was as brown as a berry, and her bright brown eyes twinkled and danced most of the time.

"I say, Mother's yelling for you to make tea," she announced to her sister, as she sauntered up to the seat.

Polly got up. "O.K. You stop here and look after Peggy."

"Oh, can't I come and help?" Peggy exclaimed, jumping up.

"Not necessary. It won't take a sec. The table's all laid, and there's only the kettle to boil. You and Lala stay here, and I'll give you a yell when it's ready." She turned and ran off to the house, leaving Peggy alone with the suddenly shy Lala, who sat down and gazed earnestly at her toes.

Not for nothing, however, had Peggy Bettany spent eleven of her sixteen and a half years at a big school, and been a form-prefect for the last one. She sat down again beside the bashful Lala, and said: "Polly's been telling me about you. You're almost my sister Bride's age, only her birthday is on the 1st of March, and yours is the end of September. What rotten luck to have your birthday just after school begins!"

"We don't go the school," Lala said, casting a quick, shy glance at her. "At Thoreston the nearest decent school was nearly seven miles away, and it would have meant the village school where you learnt nothing—except broad Yorkshire," she added, with a twinkle.

"Then how did you manage for lessons?"

"Oh, an old friend of Mother's lived in the same place. She had been a high school mistress, and Polly and I used to go to her in the mornings. Freddy, too, when he was old enough. We had prep to do in the evenings, but we always had the afternoons to ourselves. And we didn't worry too much about going home early if we were having a decent time." Two imps danced in Lala's eyes, and Peggy laughed in response to them.

"Has your mother's friend come here with you? Then what will you do now?" she asked with interest.

12

"No idea," Lala replied airily. "Isn't there a high school near?"

"At Bideford," Peggy agreed. "That would be all right, as the bus passes this house. But I have an idea that to get in you have to be about eleven, or else have been at another high school. The vicar's two girls go, and Doreen told me they're full up at present, so it mightn't be possible."

"Oh, well, I suppose the parents'll do something about it," Lala said easily.

"Perhaps they'll send you to boarding-school?"

Lala shook her head. "I doubt it! Mother had a rotten time at her boarding-school, and she's always said she wouldn't send us away."

"Oh, but if you came to our school—the Chalet School— you'd love it! No one ever has a rotten time there— unless they ask for it." Peggy spoke eagerly. "*I've* been there ever since I was a tiny, and I've loved every minute of it."

"How's that? I thought you didn't send tiny kids to boarding-school?"

"Mummy and Daddy were in India, and we lived with Auntie Madge, who owns the Chalet School more or less. She sent us all there, and David and Sybil went, too, and Josette, as well, as soon as they were old enough. They're our cousins," Peggy exclaimed. "And we weren't boarders at first—just day-girls. But when the school came to England, then we had to because Auntie's house was too far away for us in bad weather, and you couldn't always rely on the bus."

"Where *is* your school? The Chalet School, you said? That sounds rather like Switzerland. Isn't that where they have chalets?"

"Oh, anywhere in the Alps," Peggy agreed. "As a matter of fact, the school began in Tirol—in Austria, you know. That was before I was born, of course, before Daddy and Mummy were married, in fact. Then Hitler and Co. bagged Austria, so the school had to move. We went to Guernsey in the Channel Islands first, and then to the Golden Valley in Armishire, to a huge old house called Plas Howell."

Lala began to giggle. "First Austria, and then Guernsey, and now—well, Plas Howell sounds Welsh. Is Armishire in Wales?"

Peggy's blue eyes opened widely at this. "Oh, no; but it's on the Welsh border. We aren't there at the moment, though. During the Easter term something went badly wonks with the drains. We all had the most awful sore throats. So the school's had to move again until they've been put right. At present we're on a small island off the coast of Wales; St. Briavel's, It's called. We were there last term, and I rather think from what the grown-ups say that we shall be there till next summer term, anyhow. There seems to be a lot more wrong with those drains than anyone ever thought!"

"A school on an island! It sounds rather fun." Lala's brown eyes sparkled. "How do you get there? Is it very far out?"

"Oh no; we go by ferry from Carnbach, a little town on the mainland. It takes about twenty minutes or a little more to cross. It's a group of islands. Lots of them are just sea-weedy rocks; but two are used as bird sanctuaries—Kester Bellever the naturalist lives on one and is the warden for both—and there's a Dominican priory on St Bride's. St. Briavel's is the largest of the lot, and has a village, and some farms and villas besides the Big House, which is where we are for the present."

"It sounds quite decent," Lala said, after thinking it over.

"Oh, it *is*! Look here, Lala, if your mother thinks anything about sending you two away, Mummy could tell her all about the Chalet School. You'll have to go somewhere, I suppose, and I'm certain you'd love being there. It really is a wizard place."

Peggy spoke warmly, and her blue eyes glowed. Lala, looking at her, thought how pretty she was. She had tossed off her big hat when she sat down, and her hair, so fair as to be almost silvery, covered her beautifully-shaped little head with big loose rings. Her skin was as pretty as Polly's, and, thanks to her habit of wearing big hats in sunny weather, she had escaped freckles with the exception of one or two on her delicate little nose.

"And though she's so awfully fair," Lala thought, "she hasn't white eyebrows and eyelashes. I do hate those on people! They make them look like white mice! But Peggy's are dark brown, and make her eyes look the bluest things I ever saw. Yes; she *is* pretty. I wonder what her other sister is like. Young Maeve is a little picture, though she isn't in the least like Peggy."

At this point, Polly was to be heard calling them to come to tea, and Peggy jumped up at once, shaking out her skirts and picking up her hat.

"No desperate hurry. That's only Polly yelling," Lala said, rising lazily.

"I know; but it means that tea's ready. I can't very well be so rude to your mother as to go trailing in any old time the very first time I come to tea here," Peggy retorted. "She *would* think things!"

Lala said no more, but went with the new friend to the house and led her to the dining-room where tea was laid. Mrs. Winterton, a thin, worried-looking woman, was sitting at the head of the table, with Mrs. Bettany sitting beside her. Lala knew the lady by sight already, but she had never seen her quite so close, and she was greatly thrilled by her Irish beauty of eyes as blue as Peggy's, and silky black hair. She was tall, and inclined to stoutness, but when she laughed, her eyes danced with a schoolgirl merriment that made her seem very young to be mother of a girl of sixteen.

It was a very gay tea, though Polly was quiet, and took little part in the jolly chatter. After tea, the visitors took their leave after Mrs. Bettany had suggested that the Winterton family should come to tea on Saturday, when Freddy could meet Second Twins, and the girls could meet the remaining members of the family—Bride, who was away staying with friends, but would return on Friday, and the two boys, Rix and Jackie.

15

Mrs. Winterton accepted the invitation delightedly. She had been feeling very lonely since they had left Yorkshire and come to Channing St. Mary, and she had taken a fancy to this charming woman with her touch of Irish brogue, and her deep, chuckling laugh.

Lala was overjoyed, needless to state; but Polly was only half pleased. She was a queer girl, reserved, with an abrupt manner that repelled most people. Only Mrs. Bettany refused to be repelled.

"We'll be looking forward to it, won't we, Pegeen?" she said to her daughter, as they stood on the doorstep.

"Oh, rather," Peggy agreed warmly. "Give me that basket, Mummy. I'll carry it. And here's your sunshade. The sun's still blazing hot."

"True for you!" sighed her mother. "I know hot weather in India; but when England really puts her mind to it, she can rival anything there—except that we don't have the rains."

"And no snakes and horrid insects all over the place," Peggy supplemented, as they set off down the garden path. "Good-bye, Lala; good-bye, Polly. We'll see you on Saturday."

Chapter Two

THE WINTERTONS

"What did you and Peggy talk about this afternoon?"

Polly and Lala were busy in the scullery, washing up the tea-things, when Polly suddenly fired this question at her sister.

"Oh, school, and things like that. I say, Polly, do you think Mother would ever think of letting us go to the Chalet School? I thought it sounded really wizard from what Peggy said."

"I couldn't tell you. Anyhow, it'll be Father who'll settle all that sort of thing now," her sister said as she wrung out her dishcloth, preparatory to scalding it and hanging it out to dry on the lilac bush at the back door. She finished her work, and then came into the kitchen where Lala was putting away the china. "Look here, Lala; you didn't breathe a word about Lady Acetylene Lampe and all that, did you?"

"Well, as it happens, I didn't. Why not, though?"

Polly went fierily red. "Oh, well, I suppose it's rather a mad thing for girls of our age to be footling about, pretending like that. I meant to chuck it more or less when we came here, if you must know. After all, I'm fifteen now."

"*Polly*! Chuck Lady Acetylene? Oh, you *can't*! We've played it all our lives very nearly, and it's been an awful lark when things were rotten in other ways."

But Polly, nearly two years older than her sister, had felt for the past few months that the game she had invented when they were small girls, and which, as Lala truly said, they had played most of their lives, was rather beneath the dignity of a girl half-way through her teens. Above all, she couldn't bear the thought that any whisper of it should get to Peggy Bettany's ears. She felt certain that that young person would feel pretty scornful about a girl of fifteen who still played pretend games, and laugh at her. Had she only known it, she was quite wrong. Peggy was a member of a family where imagination played a big part in their lives, and had 'pretended' things just as wild or even silly as Lady Acetylene with her own young sisters and cousins. Polly, however, could not know this, and she felt that, whatever happened, she must stop Lala giving their secret away.

"I don't say I'll chuck it altogether," she said slowly, melting a little as she saw the hurt, bewildered look in her sister's eyes. All the same, young Lala, just you remember that you're not to let anyone, neither the Bettanys nor anyone else, get a sniff of it. If you do, I *will* chuck it—and

17

you with it! It's our private affair, and no one else's. So now you know!"

"Oh, I'll say nothing if that's how you feel about it," Lala responded, her face clearing. "There's Mother yelling for us. I expect she wants a walk. Let's coax her to go along to the village and watch the pilchard boats go out. I simply love seeing them spreading out across the water."

"I don't mind. Come on. If Father asks her if we kept her waiting when she called, she'll have to tell him if we do. You know how he is—a regular gimlet for questions! Scram!"

The two left the kitchen, and raced up the short flight of stairs that led to the ground floor of the house. Their mother was waiting for them in the hall, and, as they expected, suggested a walk. She agreed that it would be fun to see the pilchard fleet go out, and presently the trio were setting out, and heading for the village, which lay about a mile down the road.

Life had been a good deal changed for the Winterton family during the past year. When their father had married his second wife their home had been in a London suburb where Polly, Lala, and Freddy had all been born. When Freddy was a year old, Mr. Winterton, a well-known journalist, had been sent to the Far East as foreign correspondent for his newspaper. He had decided that his family would be happier in the country, and having inherited a big old house at Thoreston in Yorkshire, right up on the Pennine moors, a few months previously, he had persuaded his wife to agreeing to leave their villa, and move to Yorkshire with the children as soon as she could. He himself was able to do nothing more about it, as he had to be off at the end of the week.

A month after his departure, therefore, the whole family, including Giles, Mrs. Winterton's stepson, then a boy of fourteen, set off for Thoreston, where they had lived ever since. Giles was at public school then. Later, he went into the Navy, and from that time, most of his leaves were spent with friends. He was fond enough of his stepmother, who had been very good to him: but as Polly and Lala grew older, under the irregular discipline of their mother and governess, they became more and more untidy, impudent, and careless, so that he preferred to have as little to do with them as possible.

Mrs. Winterton was a fond mother, but she never could make up her mind whether to let things go or try to pull the youngsters up. Sometimes she did one thing; sometimes another. For weeks they would go on being as off-hand, disobedient, and slovenly as they chose. Then some outrageous piece of behaviour would wake up their mother, and for the next few days they were subjected to a severe discipline that might have made their lives a burden to them if they had not had ways of escaping. It never lasted, however. After a short time of this, Mrs. Winterton began to worry in case she was being too hard, and they promptly fell back into the old, slack ways.

A rude awakening for everyone had come when, after ten years abroad, the head of the house had come home, this time to give up journalism, and devote himself to writing a book he had long had in his mind. A year ago he had arrived to find his girls everything he most disliked— lazy, impudent, and disobedient. His first job must be to undo the results of the last ten years' lack of training, and it was a difficult matter. Finally he decided to cut right across their lives. They would leave the moors where they had run wild, and, sooner or later—sooner, so far as he was concerned—go to a good school where they would be under regular discipline, and learn to live with and as other girls.

He had met with difficulties from the first. The housing problem proved a very hard one, and it had not been overcome until one day in London he had met an old friend who, over the lunch they had together at their club, remarked that he was going with an exploring group to the Antarctic within a couple of months' time.

"I only heard finally this morning," he said, "and now I've got to decide what to do with my house."

Mr. Winterton pricked up his ears. "Do you mean you have a house to dispose of?" he asked.

"Well—not dispose of; not at present, anyhow. But I don't want to leave it shut up. I'd like to rent it furnished if I could find a respectable tenant who could be relied on to keep the place in order, and not walk off one fine night with all my antiques."

"Would I do?"

Dr. Swann stared. "I thought you lived in Yorkshire these days?"

"So we do; but I want to move south for various reasons. I've been trying to buy something almost ever since I returned. Look here, Swann, will you give me a three years' lease on the place? I think I can guarantee to see that your antiques are properly handled. My family is all beyond the baby stage, and, anyhow, will be away at school most of the year once I've got a house fixed up. Just whereabouts are you? Southwest somewhere, I know."

"On the North Devon coast, a mile or so from Channing St. Mary, a little fishing village, a few miles out from Bideford. You really mean it, Winterton? Good enough! We'll finish our meal, and then you can come along with me to see Corcoran—that's my lawyer. I have an appointment with him for three, so if you come along, we can get the question of the lease fixed up then and there."

Long before the expedition set off, everything had been signed, sealed, and delivered, and once he had the lease securely, Mr. Winterton broke to his family the news that he was selling their present abode, and they would move to Channing St. Mary in two months at latest. Mrs. Winterton fell in with his plans joyfully, and it was left to the girls to raise objections to the scheme, since Freddy, with prep school before him in September, cared little.

It was Polly who most resented it. Left to herself, Lala was an easy-going young person, willing to agree to anything. The strong influence her elder sister had over her had not been altogether for her good, as a result, and Mr. Winterton knew it. At the same time, he was not anxious to separate the pair altogether. He realized that the years of his absence had made his firm resolve to effect some sort of reformation in them seem harsh and

20

cruel, and he also felt that if he did as he had thought at first, and sent them to different schools, Polly, at any rate, would be long in forgiving him. So though he sternly refused to listen to his elder girl's wild entreaties to let them stay where they were, and when she became defiant and impudent, spoke so severely that even she was afraid to go on, he still meant to send them away together.

Two months after that interview with Dr. Swann, they had packed up, bringing such furniture as they most valued with them, and come to sunny Devonshire, where they had settled in at The Pantile. Things still remained uncomfortable, for Polly continued in a state of simmering rebellion the whole time; and Lala, thanks to her influence, was not much better. The previous week, things had come to a head when Polly, not knowing that her father was within earshot—spoke to her mother in such a way that he felt bound to interfere. All her bitter resentment at being taken away from the life she had known and loved, had blazed up under his rebukes, and for once she had let herself go. Lala, who was there too, became involved, and Mr. Winterton finally spoke his mind with a clarity that did put an end to their furious diatribe. He told them that unless they reformed all round, obeyed their mother with reasonable alacrity, and learned better manners and pleasanter ways, he would send them away to school—and not together. What was more, if it did come to that, he would arrange for both to remain at school for a whole year before they came home for any holidays; and if their behaviour had not been considerably amended by the end of the year, he would refuse to have them back then.

For once, even Polly was silenced, and Lala wept bitterly. But his treatment had its merit. Once they were alone together in the big attic with the unusually wide dormer window that had been given them as their room, Polly had impressed it on her sister that they must, at all costs, avoid any such separation. Since their father seemed determined to turn them into 'little ladies'—oh, the scorn Polly put into the words!—then they must do their best to comply.

Walking down the road with them, the lady pondered

on Peggy Bettany's pretty ways with her mother and politeness to herself. She knew now from Mrs. Bettany that most of Peggy's sixteen and a half years had been spent at school, and it was certain that the girl was very happy there. She wondered if this Chalet School could be quite different from St. Audries? Would it, perhaps, be a good thing for her girls if she gave in about boarding-school and let them go there? Perhaps they could try it for a term or two. She decided that she would talk it over with her husband when he came home, and if he agreed, she would go to the Quadrant and talk it over with Mrs. Bettany, to whom she had taken a great fancy. If that lady could tell her that everything was all right, and the girls would be happy there, then she would let them go. She knew what her husband had told the girls, and no more than they did she like the idea.

So deep in thought was she, that she never noticed how far they had come, and they had reached the quay, and she had nearly walked over the edge into the water if Polly had not seized her arm and yanked her back with more force than politeness.

"Good gracious, Mother!" she said crossly. "Why can't you look where you're going? You would have been in the water next minute, and there isn't a soul here to help. They're all over by the jetty. A nice mess we'd all have been in!"

"I was thinking," Mrs. Winterton said absently. Then she woke up to the situation. "Don't speak to me like that, Polly," she said. "Your father would be very angry if he heard you."

Polly dropped her arm, but the terror she had felt still lingered in her hazel eyes. "I'm sorry," she said brusquely, "but you frightened me. It's deep here, and if you'd gone in, not one of us can swim a stroke. You might have been drowned!"

In spite of the heat of the evening, Mrs. Winterton gave a shiver as she realized the danger she and the girls had been in, for she knew well enough that both would probably have plunged in to her rescue, regardless of the fact that, as Polly had said, they had never learned how to swim. "Oh, Polly," she said, "I'm sorry I frightened you, child. I really didn't know we were here. As for swimming, Mrs. Bettany suggested you should go to tea at the Quadrant on Saturday, and her two girls, Peggy and Bride, are to teach you. She says they both swim like fish—in fact, all the family do."

"Why don't you have a go too?" Lala suggested. "It would have been ghastly if you'd gone in when Polly grabbed you."

"Oh, I'm too old to begin now. But you two and Freddy shall certainly learn. Do you feel all right now, Polly? You still look white."

"I'm all right," Polly said curtly. "Come on; or we'll miss the boats setting out. They're going from the jetty."

Mrs. Winterton turned and went on with the girls, who had closed up, one on each side of her, as if determined to run no further risk with her. She glowed inwardly. Polly and Lala might not be demonstrative, but their hearts were in the right place, however much their general behaviour might need reform.

They joined the little crowd of women and children, with one or two old men, who had gathered to see the boats set sail. The small fishing cobles, with their red-brown sails glowing in the evening sunshine, stood out to sea. Slowly, as the light breeze took the sails, they bellied out, and the boats went gliding over the gently heaving surface of the water. A great herring-gull swept across the sky on powerful wings. The air was full of the murmur of the sea. Lala, quick to respond to beauty of any kind, suddenly forgot her sulks and squeezed her mother's arm.

"Isn't it *lovely*?" she said. "I do love it here!"

Her mother smiled at her. "I'm very glad. I think it's lovely too; don't you, Polly?"

Directly addressed, Polly turned to her. "Yes; it's pretty enough," she said. She turned to look after the boats, now dark patches on the gleaming waters, as they sailed out to the horizon. "There they go. Come on; let's go home. I'm hungry."

They turned away with smiles and 'good nights' from some of the women, and went back up the dusty road. Half way to The Pantile, Mrs. Winterton stopped.

"Girls," she said solemnly, "if your father will agree, how would you like to go to the Chalet School with Peggy Bettany?"

Chapter Three

A CHAPTER OF ACCIDENTS

It was the third week in September, and the members of the Chalet School were returning for the new term. To their number had been added both the Wintertons. Mrs. Bettany had privately smoothed the way for them by a long telephone conversation with the co-heads, who were close friends of her own, and when she had asked if there were vacancies for Polly and Lala, she had been told that there were.

Channing St. Mary was nowhere near a railway. The best to be done was to go to Sheepheys, the junction seven miles away, and catch the Cardiff train there. Mrs. Winterton had suggested taking the girls to St. Briavel's herself, but Mrs. Bettany had persuaded her out of the idea. They would take the party to Sheepheys, and leave them on the platform to Cardiff, after which they themselves must return by the train that had brought them unless they were prepared to spend four hours at the junction. Peggy was accustomed to looking after her sisters, and a mistress would be on escort duty at Cardiff.

"Sure, no one wants *parents* at school on the first day of term," pretty Mollie Bettany said cheerfully. "No one has any time for them. Peggy can quite well take on your pair as well as her sisters."

So it had been arranged. There was just time for the two mothers to see the girls across the bridge on to the platform for the Cardiff train, and then they had to race back to get their own. They had just vanished out of sight, when a wild shriek from Lala startled everyone within earshot.

"Mother—Peggy! Our purses! Quick! We must catch them!"

She made a dive for the steps, but Peggy was after her, and managed to grab her before she had gone more than half-way up.

"You can't catch them now! The train's moving. Come back, Lala!"

"But our purses? Mother has them, and our tickets and all our cash are in them! Whatever shall we do!" Lala turned a face full of horror on Peggy.

"Stop yelling like that, for one thing," Peggy said severely. "Everyone's looking at us. Come over here." She took Lala by the arm and marched her off to the far end of the platform, the rest of the party following.

Peggy seated herself on a convenient luggage trolley, and then demanded: "Now then, what's all this about?"

It was Polly who answered. "Father gave our purses with the journey cash and the tickets to Mother to keep for us. She's forgotten, and gone off with them, and *are* we landed!"

Peggy opened her eyes, and she whistled. "I *say*! That's a bit awkward."

"If only he'd had the sense——" Polly began; but Peggy stopped her peremptorily.

"Don't talk like that! Grousing won't help matters at all." She glanced at her watch. "Five minutes before the train's due. Bride, what cash have you?"

"Seven bob," Bride said. "How much have *you*?"

"About the same. *That* won't buy tickets to Cardiff from here. I've got Dad's cheque for the Bank, though. I wonder if it would be any use if I went and waved it round at the booking-office?"

"Shouldn't think so. It's made out to the school, isn't

it? The railway couldn't do anything with it. Still, you can *try*," Bride said hopefully.

"Well, you folk stay here with the luggage, and I'll go and see what I can do."

"You'll have to buck up. The train's due in about three minutes," Bride warned her.

"And the booking-office is on the opposite platform. Oh, bother! I couldn't do it!"

"Shouldn't we just get on the train and give the guard our names and addresses when he comes for the tickets?" Lala suggested.

"It's the ticket-collector," Peggy murmured. "It's an idea, Lala. Well, we haven't enough to get new tickets, so I suppose it's the best we can do. Here she comes! Grab your cases, and you stick to me, Maeve."

The train thundered up to the platform, and then the carriage doors were flung open. Peggy clutched her small sister by the hand, leaving Bride and the Wintertons to see to the cases, and they all scurried into a compartment where they crushed in, and Peggy, assuming command, sorted them out.

"Maeve, you can have this corner. You sit here, Lala. Bride and Polly, bag the other side. Quick, now, or you'll lose the corner seats!"

They settled down as there came a fresh influx of people, and the compartment was filled. Five minutes or so later, the train gave vent to a long hoot, and they rolled out of the station. The route was new to the Wintertons, and Lala was soon asking questions, while Bride and Polly made polite conversation about school.

When the ticket inspector came round, Peggy made her explanation, showed him her father's cheque, and gave him her home address, the home address of the Wintertons, and the address of the school. Finally, he agreed to issue the needed tickets, and left them. By the time this happened, Peggy and Polly were pink with embarrassment, and the other occupants of the compartment were eyeing them with an interest Peggy felt she could well have done without.

However, they reached Bristol safely after that, and

then the next unexpected event occurred. They were all turned out.

"What's the why of this?" Bride demanded of her sister. "We've always gone straight through to Cardiff before. Why on earth are they turning us out now?"

"You know as much as I do," Peggy retorted. "Have you all got your cases? Can you take my fiddle, Bride. I've got Maeve's belonging's to deal with. Thanks a million! Come along, Maeve!"

They finally reached the platform with all their possessions, and then Peggy had to find out from which platform the Cardiff train went. The porter she asked told her, adding a warning that they must hurry as it was at the other end of the station, and the train left in six minutes' time. He also added something about, "Mind you get in at the proper end!" but which *was* the proper end, no one could make out, as a nearby engine chose that moment for having an attack of hysterical whistling which drowned every other sound.

With the responsibility of the entire party on her shoulders, and six minutes in which to cross a bridge to the far side of the crowded and busy station and catch their train, Peggy, wisely or otherwise, decided to leave the question until they were in the train. She caught Maeve's arm with one hand, and that young lady's night-case with the other, and set off as fast as she could, the rest straggling after her, burdened with her night-case as well as their own, her fiddle, and a mixed bag of hockey-sticks, crosses and magazines. It was not easy, for various crowds were also pushing their way up or down the stairs.

However, the five reached the correct platform just as porters were banging doors. One obliging fellow picked up Maeve and put her bodily into the end carriage, and then helped the others in even as the guard blew his whistle, and the long line of carriages were on the move. Peggy had to throw the shilling she held in her hand to him. There was no time for good manners. Then, having done that, she once more took the lead and set out to seek seats, only to find that the train was crowded from end to end. Every

27

seat was filled, and people were standing in the corridors, or sitting on their cases.

"What a swizz!" Bride remarked disgustedly.

"Oh, well, it can't be helped," her sister replied. "Luckily, it isn't frightfully far to Cardiff. We'll just have to stand."

"We go under the Severn, through the Severn Tunnel, you know. I always rather hate it. It's such a long business, and I begin to wonder what would happen if the roof caved in and we got the Severn Sea on top of us." Thus said Bride, in a detached tone of voice.

"I should think we'd all be drowned," Lala said, matter-of-factly. "It hasn't ever happened, though, has it!"

"Of course not," Peggy said, overhearing this charming idea. "And it's never likely to. For one thing, it goes down deep. For another, they keep gangs of men to inspect it regularly. You need fear nothing of that kind."

"We're a long time coming to Avonmouth," Maeve said suddenly. "We gen'rally get there ages before this. What's happened, Peggy?"

"Oh, we'll be there in a minute," Peggy said.

A tall schoolgirl, wearing the uniform of a well-known school, caught this, and gave a little gasp. "I say," she exclaimed, "excuse me butting in, but are you going to Cardiff?"

"Yes," Peggy said. "Why?" Then, as the explanation broke on her, she gasped in her turn. "Oh, my godfathers! *Don't* say we've got into the wrong end of the train!"

"It's the wrong train altogether, I'm afraid," the other told her. "This is the Gloucester-Cheltenham-Hereford train. Then it goes on to Ludlow, Shrewsbury, and so to Manchester. The Cardiff train was at the other end of the platform, waiting till we pulled out," She paused. "I say! What will you do?"

Peggy groaned. "It's all the result of having to change at Bristol. We never did before. I say, Polly"—she gave a half-rueful laugh—"I'm afraid your folk will think I'm not fit to be trusted. As for what Bill and the Abbess will say to me, I just can't think!" She turned to the tall girl, who was regarding them with sympathetic brown eyes. "Can you tell me what the first stop is?"

"Gloucester," the girl said.

"Oh, thanks! I suppose we'd better get out there, find a telephone, and ring up school to find out what we'd better do. I can't think of anything else. I hope," anxiously, "we can get on from there. We haven't an awful lot of cash among us anyhow."

"I'll tell you what," said the girl. "I'm picking up my young cousin at Gloucester. This is her first term— we're at Branscombe Park, outside Ludlow—and Uncle will have brought her. There's a seven minute's stop at Gloucester. We'll tell him what's happened, and he'll see to you. I'm Nell Randolph, by the way."

"Thanks awfully." Peggy's face cleared. "That would be a help. We three," she indicated her sisters, "are the Bettanys—Bride and Maeve, and I'm Peggy. These two are Polly and Lala Winterton who are coming to the Chalet School for their first term. I'm supposed to be in charge, and *this* is what has happened!"

"I know," Nell replied. "It's hard luck. But I saw what happened, you know. That porter-lad didn't give you much chance, bunging in your kid sister like that. He never even *asked* where you were going, did he?"

"I didn't bother to think." Peggy still sounded rueful. "I saw the train standing, and took it for granted it was the Cardiff train, and just *hurtled* at it. I suppose he thought I knew. Anyhow, as you say, once Maeve was shoved in I hadn't much choice. Couldn't have her wandering round England on her own!" She exchanged grins with Maeve.

"Of course you couldn't. Anyhow, Uncle's quite a brain. He'll make it all right for you with your Head."

"Heads," Peggy corrected her. "We've got two—Miss Annersley and Miss Wilson. The worst of it is I don't quite know how we'll manage. You see, our school is on St. Briavel's—that's an island off Wales—and we go by train from Cardiff to Swansea, and then finish the journey in motor-coaches to Carnbach, where we get the ferry to

29

St. Briavel's. I don't see, after this, how we can possibly catch the motor-coaches, and our tickets don't take us further than Swansea by train."

"Oh, well, don't worry yet," Nell advised her. "Uncle will be sure to think of something." She cast a glance at the grove of hockey-sticks and crosses in the corner. "You play lacrosse at your school? I wish *we* did. I've seen one or two big club matches in London when I've been staying with Granny and Auntie Juriel, and it looks a wizard game."

"So it is! Some of the others prefer hockey; but I like lacrosse much the best," Peggy said. "I only began last year, though. You aren't allowed to take it up until you're fifteen, and the year I was fifteen I dished my ankle at tennis—I mean, it happened the summer before—so I was off games for the whole of the next two terms until it grew strong again. It's all right now, thank goodness!"

"Your school sounds rather choice," Nell said. "Branscombe Park is really awfully decent as schools go; but to be on an island, and it must be a tiny affair unless I've forgotten my map of Wales, must be awful fun. How do you manage about matches, by the way?"

"Oh, we kept up our fixtures all right last term," Peggy said. "I don't know what will happen this. You see, we used to be at Plas Howell near Howells Village in Armishire, but the drains went bad on us, so we've had to leave until they put them right. That's why we're at St. Briavel's. It only happened last term." She turned to grin at Polly. "Luck for Polly and Lala. We're rather expecting to go back to Plas Howell next year, so if they'd left it for another couple of terms, they might have missed it. As it is, they'll be in all the fun. I say, Nell, have you heard of Kester Bellever?"

"What? The bird man? Of course I have! What about it?"

"Oh, nothing," said Peggy, with a nonchalance that was decidedly overdone. "Only his bird sanctuaries are part of our island group. We know him quite well. We've

30

visited him on Brandon Mawr, and one of our girls has seen Vendell, the other one."

Nell was suitably impressed, and there was nothing to tell her that Annis Lovell had seen Vendell under conditions that had been hair-raising to a degree. Peggy kept that part of the story very strictly to herself, and even Polly knew nothing about it yet. Bride had drawn her and Lala farther away from the elder girls, and they were listening to an account of the kind of journey they would normally have had, so their elders—Nell proved to be only a month or two younger than Peggy—were able to talk freely.

They chattered happily together, and when Gloucester was coming near and the Chalet School contingent had to collect their belongings together, the two seniors were exchanging addresses, and Peggy was promising to write and let Nell know how they finished the journey.

"Though I'm certain you needn't worry," she told her new friend. "Uncle will see you through all right. He's an airman, by the way—Flight-Commander Mordaunt. He's quite a big pot in his way. He'll fix you up all right."

"It's awfully decent of you—and him," Peggy said gratefully. "I wouldn't have had this happen when I'm in charge for anything you like to name." Her eyes danced suddenly.

"What are you thinking?" Nell demanded.

"I was just wondering—but no; I don't suppose he could possibly do it," Peggy rejoined maddeningly.

"Couldn't possibly do *what*?" Suddenly Nell guessed. "Oh, if you mean *fly* you, no; he certainly couldn't! He isn't in civil aviation."

"It *would* have been wizard," Peggy said longingly. "Some of our girls have been up, and I've always longed to go, but there hasn't been any chance so far."

"Well, you certainly won't fly to-day," Nell told her. "Or not to that island of yours, anyhow. Hello! We're stopping! Oh, what a nuisance! If we're held up long,

31

we'll have next to no time for a stop, and I wanted to tell Uncle about you myself."

"Perhaps it's just a moment," Peggy said optimistically.

It proved to be three full minutes, however, and when the train finally rolled into Gloucester station, there was little time for telling anything. Nell hung out of the window, her eyes searching the crowds keenly. Suddenly she waved her hand, and the next moment the train stopped, and a tall, slim man came hurrying up to the carriage, followed by a small girl of about Maeve's age. He stood aside to let the Chalet School crowd out, but when his niece followed them, he protested.

"No, no, Nell! There isn't time! Your train's late. Here's Althea, and there's just time——"

"Oh, but Uncle, I've got to explain!" Nell protested. Then, talking at railroad speed, she told him the mess the Chalet girls were in, and enlisted his help.

He promptly promised to help them, and then bundled Nell and Althea into the carriage, where they were able to find seats. He bade them good-bye, while Peggy and her charges stood a little to one side feeling rather shy. When the train had gone, however, with Nell and her cousin waving frantically as long as they could see anyone, he turned to the five schoolgirls so unexpectedly on his hands.

"Well," he said sympathetically, "you have had a rough passage! I suppose the first thing to do is to get in touch with your school and tell them what has happened, and see if they have any suggestions to make. Come along! I've got the car outside, and we can do that sort of thing best at my house. Anyhow, it's going on for tea-time, and you'll want your tea, I'm sure. My wife will be glad to give it to you. We're going to miss Althea more than a bit, so five girls will make a good break. Here we are!" as he led them out of the station, "here's the car. Can you all squeeze in? That's right! Now we shan't be long!"

Nor were they. It had been just after three, despite his mention of tea-time, when they arrived in Gloucester, and by half-past they were seated in the drawing-room of his big flat, and Peggy was telling the story of their various mishaps in a good deal more detail than Nell had had time for. Mrs. Mordaunt chuckled over the story, and declared that her husband would put them right.

"The first thing is to ring up your school," she decided. "When that's done, we must let your people know where you are. I'm afraid, you know, that it will mean spending the night here. I don't see how else we are to manage. You certainly couldn't reach St. Briavel before midnight, even if you started out at once. Edgar,"—she turned to her husband—"suppose you take Peggy with you, and go and wrestle with the telephone. The others can come with me to the kitchen, and we'll see about tea. Bride, I wonder if you could manage to wheel my chair down the passage?"

The startled girls then realized that she was sitting in a wheel chair, though it was covered with a piece of wonderful tapestry, and looked just like a rather high armchair. Mrs. Mordaunt drew up the tapestry, showing the wheels, and sent Bride round to the back where there was a handle, and, accompanied by the others, all silent under the shock of finding this pretty, gay lady was an invalid.

Meanwhile, the Flight-Commander and Peggy had gone to the tiny room he called his study, and were wrestling with a long-distance call to St. Briavel's.

"Who should I ask for?" he demanded, while they were waiting for the connection.

"Miss Annersley," Peggy said promptly. "We have two Heads, but Miss Annersley is the chief one."

He nodded, a rather curious look on his face if Peggy had had time to notice, but just then they got through, and Peggy, sitting on the edge of the desk, heard the well-known voice of Miss Dene, the Head's secretary and general factotum, inquiring who it was. Flight-Commander Mordaunt handed the receiver to Peggy, and she was at once embroiled in an effort to explain to Miss Dene just *why* she was speaking from Gloucester.

"We've had a lot of mishaps," Peggy informed the secretary.

"I dare say! Peggy, *what are you doing at Gloucester*?"

"We got into the wrong train—we had to change at Bristol instead of going straight through, and it was a fearful scrum, and a porter pushed Maeve into the Manchester train where we met Nell Randolph. Her uncle lives in Gloucester, and he brought us to his home, and he wants to speak to Miss Annersley." Peggy managed to put the matter into a nutshell at last.

"It sounds as if you had been perfectly mad, as well as careless," Miss Dene said crossly. Then her voice changed. "Oh, Miss Annersley, Peggy Bettany is on the phone. She's speaking from Gloucester. She says they were put into the wrong train, and are now with the uncle of some friend called Nell Randolph. Will you speak? Mr. Randolph would like to speak to you."

"He isn't Mr. Randolph," Peggy interrupted; but a big hand took the receiver from her, and her host spoke.

"Edgar Mordaunt here. Is that Miss Annersley?"

Peggy heard an exclamation from Miss Annersley. The next moment she was staring wide-eyed, for her host was saying, "So it *is* you, Hilda? Somehow I thought it was when this young woman mentioned your name in connection with the Chalet School. That school had already rung a faint bell in my memory. When she said Miss Annersley was the Head, I knew where I was. Well, I haven't time to talk of our private affairs at the moment. The thing is that Peggy, her sisters, and two new girls called Winterton were put into the wrong train at Bristol by an over-zealous porter, and found themselves being carried off to Manchester. Luckily, Helen's girl, Nell, was there. Nell is Helen over again—friendly as a puppy. They chummed up, and when the train reached Gloucester where I was waiting to hand my own young Althea over to Nell to take to school with her, Nell kindly gave me these five in exchange. They are all right, and, so far as I can see, the person to blame is the porter. The thing is, what are they to do? Peggy tells me they will have missed your motor-coaches at Swansea, and I agree with her. I don't see how we are to get them to you to-night. I propose that we keep them until to-morrow, when I have to go to Swansea myself on business, and can escort them so far. Has anyone a car to collect them from there? I may say that I shall be following them along in a day or two. Now I've found you after all these years, I'm not losing you again."

Peggy heard no more, for he waved her off, and she went to look for the kitchen and help with the tea. However, when he came back to the drawing-room, it was to tell them that they were staying in Gloucester for the night. He would take them with him to Swansea next day, and Miss Annersley had promised that they would be met there by someone.

"So that's that," he wound up. "Now wire in to your tea. It would be a shame for you to be in Gloucester and not see the cathedral, so as soon as you've all had enough, I'm taking you there. Our woman comes in from six to nine, so we can manage. Don't talk; eat!"

And, as he had said, that was that!

Chapter Four

SCHOOL

"At last! Come in, young Peg, and tell us where you've been and why you've arrived a day late."

Peggy paused on the threshold of the Sixth and grinned cheerfully at her peers, who were sitting at their desks in readiness for a lesson on local government in their civics course.

"We've had a chapter of accidents," she said. "No time to tell you now; but I'll just say I'm forgiven, though a lot of it wasn't my fault. One word before Miss Dene arrives——"

"Miss Dene!" A chorus interrupted her. "It's Miss Annersley who's due."

"Civics, my love—civics!" added a stout smiling person, one Barbara Henschell. "Where's your memory gone? You *know* we stick to last year's time-table till the beginning of a full week. Always civics at this time on Wednesday."

"Better come and sit down," advised a big, fair girl with a good-tempered expression. "I saved you this desk next mine."

"Oh, thanks, Dickie." Peggy came in and occupied the desk. "And I know quite well it's civics. But it'll be Miss Dene who arrives, just the same."

"Quite right," said a fresh voice, and the form rose to its feet as a fair, pretty woman in the early thirties entered. "Miss Dene it is. Miss Annersley is engaged at present, so she sent you these questions to answer. Natalie, when the bell rings for the end of the lesson, please collect the papers and bring them to my room. Someone find me some chalk, please."

Barbara got up and produced a stick of chalk from the mistress's table, and Miss Dene wrote rapidly on the board. Then she swung the great easel round, and smiled at the girls. "Do your best," she said, and left the room.

"Oh, my stars!" Dickie groaned. What *awful* things!"

"Talking about them won't help," Peggy said austerely as she produced a sheaf of paper and her fountain pen. "I don't know who's form pree this year, but I was last. We haven't had elections yet, I suppose? O.K. Then I'm still form pree. Pitch in, everyone, and stop talking, please."

There were a few giggles, but they settled down, and giggles changed to groans as they saw what Miss Annersley had set for them.

A. Give briefly the duties of the Education Committee.
B. Mention at least five objects on which the rates are spent.
C. Explain what is meant by J.P.; Foreman of the jury; Poor Rate; M.O.H. Describe the duties of either a J.P. or an M.O.H.

Several faces fell at this formidable series of questions, and Peggy had no further need to call them to order. Once the bell rang, however, and Natalie Mensch, a dark-eyed, dark-haired slip of a girl, had collected the papers and deposited them in Miss Dene's office, they had a free period, and Peggy was besieged by questions as to what had happened.

"Wouldn't you like to know?" she said teasingly.

"Yes; we should," Dickie informed her.

"Well, one thing after another, beginning with having to change at Bristol quite unexpectedly, and about three minutes to get from one end of the station to the other, and ending up by being shoved into the wrong train and landing at Gloucester!"

"Good gracious!" an untidy-looking person interjected. "What did you do?"

"Well, luckily there was a jolly girl on the train who was picking up a small cousin to take back to school with her—kid called Althea Mordaunt—so Nell Randolph told her uncle, Flight-Commander Mordaunt, what had happened, and he took us home with him, rang up Miss Annersley, and brought us to Swansea this morning. Miss Burn met us there with the staff car, and after we'd had lunch, she brought us along. What's the time? Lunch was early—about half-past eleven—and I'm *ravenous* now!"

"It's half-past three, and you won't get any tea for three-quarters of an hour, anyhow," Barbara Henschell told her.

"Oh, dear! Well, tell me the news, and I may be able to hang out."

"Yes; there *is* news—piles of it!" Natalie responded. "To begin with, all of last year's Sixths have departed. The only ones left are Jean Mackay, Eilunedd Vaughn, Pamela Whitlock, Jean MacGregor, and Anthea Barnett, who are all in Special Sixth, and the six you see here who were part of Lower Sixth last term. Anyhow, Dickie was new, and so was Gwen Evans. That would have left only four of us for Upper Sixth, so for this term, anyhow, we're all to be together."

Peggy flopped into the nearest chair. "That *is* news! Any idea who's likely to be Head girl?"

Natalie shook her head. "Nor has anyone else. It won't be anyone in Special Sixth, anyhow. Bill said never again after Marilyn Evans made such a mess of it the year before last. It'll be one of us, I suppose; but who, I've no idea."

Peggy sat up alertly. "I can tell you who it *won't* be!"

"Oh? Who, then—and why?"

"Joan Sandys! It's no use looking like that, Joan. You know as well as I do that you're *the* person for games."

Joan, a plump, capable-looking girl, flushed. "What rot! Nita is quite as good as I am—or Barbara Smith—or Judy Rose—or yourself, come to that. Your tennis is super, and you play a very pretty crosse when you like."

"*And* I'm very little use at hockey, and an also-ran at cricket. Nita scores there; but she doesn't play lacrosse—"

"Never cared for it," interposed Nita Eltringham, a slender person, with wide-apart grey-green eyes, and a small oval face framed in a mop of fluffy brown hair. "You can count *me* out for games, Joan, on that score alone. Peggy's right about you, you know. You're the best all-rounder we have. Games are your highlight. Look at the way you came on at rowing last term, when you'd never touched an oar in your life before! I don't know about the other jobs; but you're a cert for the games."

Joan went redder, but the rest gave her no chance to speak. Joan, to their minds, was the ideal person to be Head of the games. As for what Nita had called "the other jobs", they must wait until the name of the Head Girl had been given. So far, no one had the remotest idea who it was likely to be.

"I wish it was fine," Barbara sighed, staring out of the window at the fine drizzle that was wetting everything thoroughly. "I could just do with a good walk now before tea!"

"Not a chance in weather like this," laughed pretty Judy Rose.

The door opened, and the Sixth got to its feet in a hurry, for no less a person than Miss Annersley entered.

She was a tall, slenderly built woman; not pretty, but with a fine face, lighted by a pair of blue-grey eyes which had never yet needed glasses. Her glossy brown hair was brushed back from a broad brow, and twisted into a 'bun' on the back of her neck. Her pleated skirt and blue jumper, were all immaculate. Though so tall, she carried herself beautifully, and the girls gave her not only respect, but a warm affection. Therefore, the greeting she received from them was a cordial one. She was a very busy person, and apart from her lessons with them, she had not much spare time for ordinary chatting, though every girl in the school knew that if she wanted the Head, she would find her in the study between six and seven, and no matter what she was doing, she was ready to set everything on one side and give her mind to the needs of any pupil.

"Well," she said, as she sat down in the big chair Nita pulled forward for her, "I haven't had any time so far to have a talk with you. I've got tea-time free, however, so I came to see if you Sixth Formers would care to come along and have it with me at half-past four. We have a good deal to discuss, I think, and it'll be more comfortable over tea and scones." She turned to Peggy. "Peggy, I haven't really had a chance to see you yet. I'm sorry you had such a worrying time yesterday. However, it's turned out well—*very* well, all things considered. But another time, do find out about your trains before you set out!"

"Yes, Miss Annersley," Peggy said, going scarlet. Out of school the Head was 'Auntie Hilda'; but in school the girls to whom she accorded the use of this title were very careful not to use it.

"Miss Annersley, please have you any idea who is to be Head Girl?" Natalie asked anxiously. "We want to get on with prefect jobs, but until we know that we can't do a thing."

The Head laughed. "Of course I know. So will you at tea-time: not until, however. Don't *moo* at me girls! It won't hurt you to wait another half-hour or so." Her eyes twinkled as she surveyed their faces. Then she got up. "I'll just say one thing. I think you're all going to get a shock over it—especially the chosen one. Now I'm going. Be with me at half-past four sharp."

She gave them another smile, and left them all agog with curiosity.

"What on earth can she mean?" Nita cried, as soon as the door had closed on her. "*Who* have they chosen for Head Girl this time?"

"Daphne Russell, perhaps," suggested someone.

"Oh, rot!" retorted that individual forcefully. "I'm the youngest in the form, and only got in by the skin of my teeth. Is it *likely* anyone's going to choose me for Head Girl? Do use your sense, Nina!"

"What's the matter with our Frances, then?" suggested Dicky Christy. "If Daphne's the youngest, she's the eldest——"

"I'm not, then; that's Barbara," Frances said placidly. "And *no* one would choose me. I'm too much of a SHOCKING EXAMPLE. Matey would have a lot to say in that case."

"Where are you off to, Peg?" Natalie Mensch demanded, as Peggy suddenly jumped up from her seat on the floor.

"I've just remembered I've two new girls to be responsible for, and I've seen nothing of them since we came. I'll just take a dekko at them to be sure they're all right, and come back. It'll be about time for tea with the Abbess by that time."

Peggy waved to them, and vanished, and they turned once more to the big question of the hour.

Meantime, Peggy herself went running along the corridor, and down the stairs till she came to the Senior common-room. She opened the door and peeped in. Her own sister was sprawled out in an armchair near the window, but otherwise the room was deserted.

"Hello," Peggy said. "Where's everyone?"

"At gym. Matey grabbed me for unpacking," Bride explained. "I've just finished, and she sent me in here. The others'll be along shortly. What've you been doing?"

"Civics test—ghastly one too! I'll have to unpack after tea. Where are Polly and Lala?" Peggy demanded.

"With Miss Slater, being put through form tests, poor lambs," Bride grinned. "I say, Peg, won't it be weird not to have Miss Burnett or Linny any more? They've been here donkeys' years. We're going to miss them."

"It won't be so bad about Linny," Peggy said. "After all, she and Mr. Young are living near Plas Gwyn. But Miss Burnett is going to Aberdeen, and that's quite a journey."

"Who's taking history? Have you heard yet?"

"There hasn't been time. We've been discussing who's to be Head Girl."

"Anyone know?"

"The Head; but she's not telling just yet."

"Oh, well, we'll hear all the news at tea."

"I shan't be there." Peggy said this with some satisfaction.

Bride sat up in surprise. "You won't be there? Then where will you be if I may ask?"

"Having tea with Auntie Hilda. She's just been in to ask us—the whole form, I mean. So you'll hear from the others, and I expect we'll hear from her. I'll have to go and make myself fit to be seen. Keep an eye on Polly and Lala, will you. It's just till they find their feet a bit."

"O.K., I don't mind," Bride agreed amiably. "All the same, judging from what they've both said, I rather imagine they won't be in my form, not even Polly. I rather think she'll get into Lower Fifth with a scrape, and Lala one of the Fourths. If it's Upper, I'll tackle young Sybs, and she can look after her. If it's Lower, well I don't know much about that crowd. Wendy Robson'll be there, won't she? She's a good-natured kind of kid, and I expect she'd do it. You know," she went on confidentially, "I think young Lala will be all right; but I rather think it'll take Polly a time to shake down."

"What makes you think that?" Peggy asked, startled at her young sister's prescience.

"I don't know; just a feeling I've got."

41

Peggy slipped into one of the Splasheries, as the school called their cloakrooms, and washed her hands and face, and drew a pocket-comb through the fair curls tied back from her face. Then, having made certain that her blouse and skirt were all that could be wished, she raced upstairs.

The Sixth were all ready, and once the tea-bell for the school at large had rung, and the feet of the last girl had been heard entering the dining-room, they paired off, and, walking demurely, went down to the pretty room which was shared by both Heads, very eager to hear what had been decided about the Head Girl and prefects.

"Although some of us were junior prees last year, so we're fairly safe to be seniors this," Joan Sandys remarked as they left the room.

As rules about talking on the stairs were strict, no one could reply to this. Even if most of them were neither junior prefects nor subs, all were Seniors, and as such, expected to keep to rules.

In the pretty sitting-room, they found Miss Annersley seated at a lavish tea-table, and Miss Wilson, her co-Head, curled up in the window-seat. Peggy made a bee-line for her at once.

"Auntie Nell," she said eagerly, "it's lovely to see you!"

Miss Wilson, "Bill" to most of the school, laughed. "It's not six weeks since I was staying at the Quadrant. We were with you for Gillian Linton's wedding," she reminded the girl. "And be careful, Peggy. We agreed that I was to be 'Miss Wilson' in term-time."

"No one's listening," Peggy assured her.

"That's true. Well, I suppose you're all aching to know about the Head Girl and prefects. Come and sit down."

Miss Annersley dispensed tea, and saw that everyone was supplied with scones.

"Well, I see that you aren't going to enjoy your meal until you hear all about our latest arrangements, so you shan't be kept in suspense any longer. Miss Wilson has the prefect list, and will read it to you at once. Of course, former prefects now in Special Sixth will act when they are needed; but, as you know, their time-table makes it difficult for them to be with you girls as much as is needful for prefects. That is why we always choose most of the important posts from among members of the Sixths. As you know, also, we lost an unusually large number of elder girls at the end of last term, so for the present we have decided to amalgamate Upper and Lower Sixth. I am not sure," she added, "that we shouldn't have had to do something of the kind in any case just now. It is very difficult to get staff and we lost three members of the staff, too, last term."

"Aren't we having new mistresses, then, Miss Annersley?" Judy Rose asked.

The Head was silent for a moment. Then she spoke. "We have a new mistress for junior history, who will also teach some of Miss Linton's subjects; and, of course, we have a new handcrafts mistress in place of Miss Carey. That is all, though."

"But who's going to take our history?" Daphne asked anxiously.

"Well," the Head said slowly, "we have a visiting mistress coming twice a week for the Upper Fourth and the three Fifths."

"And what about us?" Dicky Christy demanded. "Aren't we to do history at all?"

"Oh, I hope it isn't that!" Peggy cried. "I love history."

The two Heads looked at each other, and for no reason that the eager girls could see, both suddenly chuckled. Then Miss Wilson had mercy on them.

"Of course you are going on with history. Don't be so silly! As for who is going to teach you, well, what do you say to—Joey Maynard?"

"Mrs. Maynard?"—"Joey!"—"Auntie Jo!"

The girls all spoke at once, but Peggy's cry of "Auntie Jo!" pealed out above the others.

Miss Annersley nodded. "Yes; Mrs. Maynard."

"But how can she?" Peggy asked, wide-eyed. "She lives at Howells Village, and it takes ages to get here."

"As it happens, Peggy, your aunt is leaving Plas Gwyn

for the present," the Head told her. "No; it isn't drains like Plas Howell. It's something almost as alarming, though. Part of the foundations has begun to subside, and the house isn't safe. Mercifully, they can manage to get it set right, but it means demolishing one end and rebuilding, which is likely to prove a lengthy job. Commander Christy offered Jo a house in Carnbach which is his, and which has just fallen vacant. So she will be there for the next two terms, anyhow. It all depends on what sort of winter we have whether the rebuilding can be finished then or not. If it's a severe winter, then she will probably be here until the summer."

"Well," said Daphne, "I'm awful sorry for Mrs. Maynard having all that bother, but I must say I think it's wizard for us!"

"Oh, so do I!" Nina Williams cried. "I can just imagine her being a super history teacher. I do think we're in luck to have her."

"Why isn't Auntie Jo teaching all the senior history?" Peggy asked.

"Because she couldn't possibly spare the time," Miss Wilson said promptly. "Stephen only goes to morning school, and then there are Charles and Michael."

"Will Steve come here, then, with Len and Con?" Peggy asked thoughtfully.

"No; there's a nice little kindergarten school in the same road as the new house, just five minutes' walk away, and he'll go there."

"Well, anyhow," Dicky summed it up, "it's marvellous having Mrs. Maynard around, and I can't think why Dad didn't tell me. He heard me wondering what was going to happen now that Miss Burnett has married her doctor at last, and he never said squeak!"

"What's the house like, Dicky?" Daphne asked.

"If it's the one I think it is—Dad owns three in Carnbach—it's quite a decent affair, standing by itself in a jolly garden. I think it's almost bound to be Cartref."

"Quite right," Miss Wilson said. "It is Cartref."

They continued to discuss the new arrangements until

tea was ended, and when it was over, the bell rang for preparation before they had heard anything about the prefects.

"Oh," Natalie implored the two Heads, "we've got to go, as most of us are on prep duty; but please, *do* tell us who is to be Head Girl before we go."

Miss Annersley smiled at their anxious faces. "I shall tell the school after prayers to-night. You people should know first, but please don't broadcast it."

"Oh no!" they agreed fervently.

"Then," she said, "here is the prefect list." She turned to her partner and friend. "Read it to them."

Miss Wilson produced the list from the pocket of her cardigan, and read out: "Senior prefects: Peggy Bettany —Mollie Carew—Dicky Christy—Frances Coleman—Nita Eltringham—Barbara Henschell. Junior prefects: Judy, Rose—Daphne Russell—Nina Williams. Games prefect Joan Sandys. Head girl, Peggy Bettany."

A gasp went up from the listening group of fifteen girls at the last announcement. As for Peggy herself, her eyes and mouth were round with surprise. Miss Wilson exchanged a swift glance of amusement with Miss Annersley before she continued: "These names will be given out to the school. After that, the prefects had better have a prefects' meeting to distribute the various duties."

"Now you must go," Miss Annersley chimed in. "Peggy, I think you are not on duty. Will you remain for a few minutes. I want to speak to you."

Before Peggy could say yea or nay, Dicky Christy and Daphne Russell had grabbed her hands, and were wishing her a good year as Head Girl. The rest followed their example. Then they fled to take over duty, generally a strenuous affair during the first prep or two of the term. Miss Wilson, who had certain affairs of her own, also departed, and Peggy, still wondering if it was really Peggy Bettany on that settee, was left alone with Miss Annersley to hear what that lady had to say to her.

Chapter Five

HEAD GIRL PEGGY

Miss Wilson had left the room with the other girls, and only Miss Annersley was left with Peggy. She looked across the room at the girl as the door closed behind Nina Williams, the last to leave, and gave her a smile.

"Well, Peggy? You look very startled, child. Surely you must have realized that you were well in the running for Head Girl?"

"But I didn't," Peggy said slowly. "For one thing, though we all knew that people like Gay, and Jacynth, and Kathie were leaving, none of us expected such a—a *wholesale* clear-out as there's been. I mean Lavender Leigh, and Doreen O'Connor, and Mary Everitt, and people like that one expected to stay on till next summer. I did think I might be a prefect; but I rather thought Mary Everitt would be Head Girl. Lots of the others are older than I, Auntie Hilda, and Dicky, Natalie, Frances, Gwen, and Barbara were all in Lower Sixth last term."

"Well," Miss Annersley said, "like you, I didn't expect such a clear-out. Lavender has been an uncertain quantity for the last year, so I wasn't too surprised when Miss Leigh wrote finally to say she was not coming back this term. Doreen is going to the University, and only stayed on until there was a vacancy. She's past eighteen, you know—very nearly nineteen. As for Mary, Mr. Everitt was offered a good post in Kenya, and the whole family are going almost at once."

"But there are the others who *have* stayed on," Peggy argued.

"I know; but Natalie is specializing in music this year,

with a view to training for concert work. She doesn't know it yet, but she is going to Special Sixth next week. Dicky and Gwen were new last term and not even prefects. As for Frances and Barbara, Frances will make a good Senior prefect, but she would be the first to beg off the Head Girl business, and Barbara is a good, conscientious girl, but she wouldn't do for Head Girl, either. No, Peggy; it has to be you."

Peggy looked mutinous. "I haven't been a prefect, either, yet."

The Head nodded. "I know that. Neither have any of the others of your set."

"But why pitch on me?" Peggy was upset. "I mean, I'm no better than any of the others. We were all sure that Joan would get Games. She's the best all-round, and she's a good organizer too. That knocked her out for Head Girl."

"Yes; there was never any question as to who should take over the Games," Miss Annersley agreed, watching the fair face closely. "And when I discussed the Head Girl, you may like to know that it was practically a unanimous choice for you. Now listen to me, Peggy, and try to understand. As you have pointed out, we are left with very few former Sixths this year. Most of those left are specializing and are therefore in Special Sixth. As you know, we had a member of Special Sixth for Head Girl two years ago, and it didn't answer. Marilyn was working very hard, and she has always been very ambitious. When it came to a choice as to whether her own work or the school must go to the wall, in a great many cases it was her own work that won, and the school suffered. We decided then that it was fair to neither the school nor the girls to ask such a thing of Special Sixth and it should not happen again. That, in view of the fact that Dickie and Gwen have had only one term with us, and neither Frances nor Barbara could be really happy or successful in such a post, left us with a choice of one of you people who have come up from Upper Fifth. On all counts, the lot had to fall on you—

and I hope you are going to justify our choice," she added, with a brilliant smile.

Peggy still looked troubled. "It isn't that I'm not thrilled about it. Part of me is awfully bucked at the idea," she confessed. "But I've had no real experience, and I'm afraid I may make an awful mull of it."

"You've been Form prefect in every one of the forms you've been in for the last four years," Miss Annersley said swiftly. "I don't suppose you ever realized that that in itself is a training for prefectship; but it is. You've shown us that you can organize successfully, and that you can handle other girls well." Then, as Peggy still looked downcast, she added: "Come, Peggy! The school has given you a good deal all these years. Are you going to refuse what it asks of you now?"

"Oh, it isn't that!" Peggy cried, her face going crimson. "But—well, look at the Head Girls we've *had*! Gill Culver and Jacynth Hardy; and before them, Beth Chester and Robin Humphries; and Elizabeth Arnett; and away back in Tirol there were Hilary Burn, and Gillian Linton, and Jo, and Mary Burnett, and—oh, all the others!"

"You mentioned your Aunt Jo. Well, you were only a very small child at the time, so I doubt if you ever realized that she begged even harder than you are doing to be excused the job."

Peggy sat up. "*Jo* did! But—but I've always heard she was one of the best Head Girls we ever had!" she cried loudly.

"So she was. Nevertheless, if she *could* have wriggled out of it she would have. Only, luckily for everyone, no one would listen to her. And it was another Head Girl who finally succeeded in reconciling her to her fate. I mean Gisela Mensch, our first Head Girl."

"Natalie's mother? I know *she* was one of them. But Auntie Jo! It doesn't seem possible!" Peggy marvelled.

"Oh, more than possible." Miss Annersley still spoke drily. "Like yourself, Jo had never expected to be Head Girl—or not so soon, anyhow. Mary Burnett had been, and should have stayed on till the end of the summer term; but Mrs. Burnett had an accident, and there were two small boys who were one person's work at home, so Mary had to leave school a term sooner than anyone expected, and Jo was appointed."

Peggy's eyes sparkled as the Head, in the interest of former days, forgot to speak formally, and alluded to her aunt as simple "Jo"; but she said nothing.

"Jo was terribly upset," Miss Annersley continued. "She told us quite frankly that she'd planned to have a gorgeous summer term, and now here she was, landed with Head Girl! She hated the idea. She spent the whole of the Easter Holidays in a state of rebellion, and your Aunt Madge was at her wits' end to know what to do with her. She told me later that she had even thought the idea must be given up, and either Frieda Mensch or Marie von Eschenau appointed in her place. And then one evening Jo went to see Natalie, who was a baby of a few weeks old, and came back more or less resigned. She never looked back after that."

The Head moved in her chair, and she looked straight at the girl near her. "If you really hate the idea so much that you will make yourself miserable about it," she said abruptly, "I suppose we must think it over. But I hope it won't come to that."

It was Peggy's turn to look thoughtful. Miss Annersley made no attempt to hurry her. She picked up a piece of knitting that lay in the chair behind her, and began to count her stitches. Presently Peggy stood up.

"I—it's a fearful shock, Miss Annersley," she said, using the more formal mode of address in her earnestness, "but if you do all really think I can do it—I'll have a stab at it: and I'll do my best."

The Head nodded. "I thought you'd say that when you'd had time to think it over," she said. "Ring the bell for Megan to clear these crocks away, will you, Peggy? And then you ought to go and do something about your prep, or you'll get nothing done to-night."

Peggy rang the bell and went to the door, where she turned to make the curtsy that was traditional in the

Chalet School, dating from Tirol days, when so many of the girls had been continentals with the continental training in good manners.

Peggy, still feeling rather as though she were walking on her head, made her way back to the Sixth Form room where such of her compeers as were not on duty with junior or middle preparation were busy with their own work. As she entered, looking and feeling self-conscious to a degree, pens were dropped, books were pushed aside, and the girls eyed her with welcoming grins.

"See the conquering heroine comes!" Judy Rose chanted.

Poor Peggy flushed. "Oh, for pity's sake don't rag me! I can't see why on earth they should have chosen *me*——"

"Maybe not; but we can," Hester Layng, a lazy young person, who always did the minimum of work in whatever form she adorned, retorted. "Well, rather you than me! I should say being Head Girl's an awful sweat, whatever honour's attached to it."

Barbara Henschell chuckled. "Grapes sour, Hester?"

"Not in the least! Thank goodness I'm not even a sub, let alone Head Girl," Hester replied sweetly. "Peggy, we all wish you the best luck in the world, and we're all awfully glad it's you."

"That's true," Barbara nodded.

The rest chimed in, and Peggy began to feel happier.

"It's jolly decent of you people," she said. "I'll do my best, you may be sure. And now," with a determined changing of the subject, "will someone kindly tell me what prep we have so far? Remember I missed most of to-day's lessons."

They told her, and when she had scribbled it down, she glanced at the clock above the mantelpiece. "Well, we've little more than an hour left, so we'd better get down to it. Taisez-vous!"

"We will; but just one question, Pegs," Barbara pleaded. "When do we have prefects' meeting?"

Peggy got up to go and scan the time-table. "I think

50

we're all free to-morrow afternoon," she said finally. "Three o'clock to-morrow in the prefects' room suit you all?"

No one objected, so she scribbled a notice, ran downstairs to put it on the big notice-board in what had once been the drawing-room of the Big House as it was properly called, and then returned to do what she could with the French essay on *Une patrie je voudrais voir*, which it had pleased Mlle de Lachennais, the senior French mistress, to set them.

Work, however, was not to be for Peggy that evening. She had just finished her first paragraph, when there came a knock at the door, followed by the entrance of a pig-tailed twelve-year-old.

"What do you want, Mary-Lou?" she asked.

"You, please, Peggy," Mary-Lou replied. "You're wanted downstairs by a—a lady." Her cheeks were suspiciously pink, and she avoided a giggle only by a miracle.

"Oh, bother!" Peggy exclaimed. "I'll never get this thing done! Very well, Mary-Lou, I'm coming. Off you hop back to work!"

Peggy went slowly down the stairs, wondering who on earth could be wanting her now. She entered a small room to the right of the front door, and then stopped short.

"Auntie Jo!" she exclaimed. "Oh, Auntie Jo, how simply *wizard*!"

The tall, dark lady, who had been standing at the window, looking out at the soaking garden, whirled round, and caught her hands.

"Let's have a look at you, Peg!" she cried, holding the girl away from her for a moment before she bent to kiss her. "Congratulations, my lamb! The very first of the second generation to be Head Girl! Aren't we proud! At least," she added as she pulled Peggy down on to a settee near the window, "I *am*, and your mother *will* be shortly, for I'm ringing her up this very night as soon as I get home to tell her. I'm cabling Auntie Madge too Won't Margot and Josette and Ailie be bucked to think they're cousins of the new Head Girl! And won't Auntie Madge get a thrill! Well, how do you feel about it?"

"Completely mazed," Peggy told her. "I never expected it for a moment, and I still don't see what sort of a fist I'll make at it."

"An excellent one, of course! Talk sense, Peg! As for mazed, you ought to be hopping with joy. It's a fearful honour, my good kid."

"Ye-es. And did *you* feel it a fearful honour when they appointed *you*?" Peggy asked slyly.

Her aunt chuckled. "Who's been telling tales out of school? You know perfectly well I did *not*. I'd planned a simply wizard term, with all sorts of fun and games for myself and the rest, and there I was—landed! Oh, I set up a howl all right! But then, if you've heard anything about me at school, you must know that I wasn't exactly a peaceful character in those days. I've improved considerably since then," she added complacently.

Peggy gave a peal of laughter. "It's as well you think so! Auntie Jo, you *know* that there are times when you'd give your ears to be a schoolgirl again among us all. But you can't! You're Mrs. Maynard now and the proud mother of six—Help! Doesn't it sound a crowd when you say it like that?" she added.

"Well, that comes well from you!" Jo Maynard cried indignantly. "You're one of six yourself if it comes to that!"

"I know; but we *have* stopped at Second Twins. I wouldn't put it past you to go on and have a few more. Michael's fourteen months old now. In another year's time you'll be saying you miss having a baby just as you did when Charles was about two, and then you'll have one."

"Quite likely," her aunt said calmly. "I like big families. I was an only child myself to all intents and purposes. Your father and Aunt Madge were twelve years older than I. Madge brought me up, in fact, bless her! However, we'll leave me out of it at the moment. Anyway, I've only ten minutes more to spare for you to-day. David Griffiths brought me over in his boat, and I'm catching the ferry back, so I daren't stay too long. I simply had to come to see you, though. Next week you'll be having me twice a week for history," she added. "Had you heard that?"

Peggy nodded. "Miss Annersley told us so. She had all our crowd to tea. You've heard what happened on the journey, haven't you?" she added.

"That was one of the things I heard over the phone. Also that your Flight-Commander Mordaunt is a distant cousin of Miss Annersley's whom she hadn't seen for years. They used to be chums when they were younger; then he went out to Canada to train, and they lost touch somehow. I can tell you she was wildly excited about it when she rang me up."

"Not really? I say! What a coincidence!" Peggy was suitably impressed. Then she went back to her own doings. "Auntie Jo, you're coming over twice a week. If I get into any messes, can I come to you?"

"Yes; if it's really something you can't handle for yourself," Jo said promptly. "But stand on your own feet, Peg, if you can. You will find that it's always wiser." She glanced at her watch. "Heavens! I must go! Don't tell the kids I've been, for I haven't asked to see them. I knew there wouldn't be time, and I delivered them only yesterday. I've warned Mary-Lou about that. Oh, and you'd better say nothing to Sybil, either. I'm having you and Bride and Maeve, and Sybs on Saturday as I said. I've got some news for you all." She made a face.

"Isn't it good news?" Peggy asked anxiously.

"From one point of view it is not—definitely not! From another I suppose it's all right. You'll understand when I tell you. Now I must go. Good-bye, my Peggy-girl. Thank goodness I'll be seeing lots of all you folk this term! Hope it'll be a good term for you and everyone. Kiss me, and let me go!"

Peggy did as she was asked, and Mrs. Maynard grabbed her bag from the table on which she had tossed it, left the house, and went racing down the drive more like the schoolgirl Péggy had accused her of wanting to be than, as that young woman had said, the mother of six.

Left to herself, Peggy went back upstairs, but she had just reached the top step when the bell rang, and prep was over.

"Oh, goodness! And I haven't done a stroke of real work!" she thought, as she went on to put her books away. "All the same, I feel a lot better about everything. Auntie Jo's just super!"

"Who wanted you, Peggy?" Hester demanded as she entered the room.

"Just what Mary-Lou said—a lady," Peggy replied serenely. "Hurry up, folks! Some of us are prefects now, and it won't look well if we trail in for prayers any old time."

The girls left the room, and filed quickly down the stairs. Girls were everywhere, including Bride Bettany, with Polly beside her. Lala was in tow with a red-head of about her own age, one Clemm Barras, who was famed for being one of the most irrepressible people who had ever come to the school. Talking was strictly forbidden, so Peggy could only grin companionably at the new girls on her way to Hall, as the big drawing-room was now called. It had two doors, and ran right across the house from the front door to the far end. The girls entered by the lower door and the notice-board hung between the two windows at the side of the house, so though they could see one notice against the green baize, no one could read it, and no one was daring enough to go to see what it was. Only the Protestant girls had prayers here, the Catholics having their own little service with Miss Wilson in the inner drawing-room, which opened off the large room. The Sixth Formers made their way to the top of the room where a low platform had been set on which stood the school lectern, and chairs for the staff, with a piano at one side. For to-night, the entire form, together with the stately damsels from Special Sixth, would stand at one side. Once the prefect lists had been read out, however, what Daphne Russell called the hoi polloi

54

would go to stand at the back of the room behind the rest, and Special Sixth would go with them.

There was very little noise in the room. Silence was not imposed until the second bell had gone, but everyone knew that after prayers they would learn the names of the prefects and the Head Girl, and even the small folk were impressed with the importance of the occasion.

Standing in her place between Dickie Christy and Daphne Russell, Peggy looked steadily at the girls. She cast a cousinly smile at her younger cousin, Sybil Russell —Daphne was a friend, and no relation—and then looked at the long rows of juniors, where Jo Maynard's two elder girls, Len and Con, were standing very erect, and side by side. They and the sister who was with their Aunt Madge in Canada were triplets, and until the spring had never been separated in their lives. Well, thought Peggy as she waved to them, October would soon be here, and Auntie Madge with her own two younger girls, Josette and Ailie, and Margot, the third triplet, would be at home. It would be wizard to see them all again, especially Aunt Madge. Peggy and her twin brother and Bride had been left behind in Tirol with the Russells when the twins were four and Bride only three, and Lady Russell had been mother to them until Mr. and Mrs. Bettany had come home for good from India, which had happened three years ago. Peggy loved her parents very dearly, but Aunt Madge was something very special for all that!

The second bell rang, and the little rustling of low chatter ceased as the staff came in, with Miss Annersley last of all. She took her place on the dais, and gave out the number of the hymn. Miss Cochrane, head of the music, played the first line of Bishop Ken's Evening Hymn, and the girls sang it. Then the Head read the twenty-third psalm. Prayers followed—Our Father—Gentle Jesus for the little ones—Lighten our darkness—and the blessing. A minute's silence, and they rose to their feet as the dividing doors opened, and the Catholics came in, while Miss Wilson and two or three mistresses joined the others on the dais.

"Sit down, girls," Miss Annersley said, when they were all there.

They sat down on the floor, and the Head looked down on the rows of bright faces uplifted so eagerly to hers.

"I won't keep you long, girls," she said, her beautiful deep voice reaching clearly to the farther end of the room. "I am just going to tell you the names of the new prefects, the Head of the Games, and the Head Girl, and then you must go to supper after Miss Wilson has pinned the badges on our chosen leaders."

She paused, and Peggy, fumbling with the little bar brooch that kept her tie in place, felt acutely several people round her doing the same, even as the Head went on to make the explanation she had given the Sixth Form at tea. She did not mention Marilyn Evans or the fiasco she had made of the post, though she reminded them that Special Sixth, being very busy people, were not included among the school prefects, though in case of need they would act as such, and must be treated as such.

"And now," she concluded, "as I know you are all longing to hear whom we *have* chosen, I will read out the names, and the new prefects will please come up as I name them to receive their badges."

"Mollie Carew," read Miss Annersley; and Mollie, the colour of beetroot, edged past the others, and went up to have her badge fastened in her tie by Miss Wilson, while the school clapped loudly.

"Frances Coleman!"

Bride, among the Upper Fifth, looked round indignantly. It was the rule of the school that the prefects' names were called in alphabetical order. In that case, Peggy should have come first. Of course, she had never been even a *junior* pree or a sub, but neither had Mollie Carew. Surely she wasn't going to be left out!

The reading went on. One after another the chosen prefects went up to get their badges and be applauded by the school. When Judy Rose, the last, had gone blushingly to her place, there was another little rustle. Who was to have Games? Who could possibly be Head Girl?

A faint hope suddenly swelled in Bride, making her almost breathless. Could it possibly be that *Peggy* was to be IT?

"But however could she do it?" thought the younger sister. "She hasn't had any *experience!*"

"Games prefect, Joan Sandys," Miss Annersley read; and the school cheered. Joan was a popular person, and most of the seniors, at any rate, had expected this.

She went up for her badge, looking very startled at her reception. She was a humble-minded person on the whole, and had had no idea of her universal popularity.

"Head Girl"—Miss Annersley made a little pause; then she finished—"Peggy Bettany."

There was a stunned silence for a moment. Then the cheering broke out afresh as Peggy, rivalling even Mollie in her blushes, went to receive the little silver shield which bore the words "Head Girl" in flame-coloured enamel across it.

Above the cheering, a clear high voice was to be heard.

"Good for Peggy! Told you so, Phil Craven! Hooray, Peggy!"

"Oh, *drat* that Mary-Lou!" Peggy thought viciously, as with scorching cheeks she stood while tall Miss Wilson bent her head with its crown of snowy, curling hair to see what she was doing. The badge was safely in the flame-coloured tie at last, and then Miss Annersley touched Peggy to make her turn to the girls and to thank them.

The cheering died down as the Head Girl faced the school, and they waited to hear what she would say. Peggy swallowed once or twice. Then in a curiously high voice which only just did not shake with nervousness, she said: "Thank you very much, all of you. I'll do my best." After which she was allowed to leave the dais and slip, for the last time, into the ruck of her form. Hereafter, she must stand at the head of the prefects, and nearest to Miss Annersley, ready to take any message or bring anything.

The Heads gave the girls free rein with their excitement for a minute. Then Miss Wilson said something in an undertone to Miss Stevens, who was behind her, and Miss

57

Stevens nodded and slipped out. The next moment the supper-gong was ringing, and they all knew that it was a signal that the noise must cease, and they must march out to supper in the dining-room.

Peggy had to endure a good deal of patting on the back, and many congratulations once they were in the dining-room, but by this time she was beginning to feel her feet, and was able to cope.

"Good for you, Peggy," said Anthea Barnett of Special Sixth, a pretty girl who was going in for art needlework, and was only staying at school until there should be a vacancy for her at a famous School of Art Needlework. "I'm very glad they chose you."

Eilunedd Vaughn, another member of the same form, a small, very dark Welsh girl, gave the Head Girl a peculiar glance. "Oh yes; no doubt Peggy *will* do very well," she said. "She has so much to help her. Brought up in the tradition of the school from the moment of your birth, weren't you, Peggy?"

Peggy was too excited to notice the inwardness of this. She laughed. "Not *quite* that, but very nearly. Thanks, Anthea and Eilunedd." She turned then to answer a remark made by Judy Rose, and forgot it. Only Dickie Christy, sitting next to her, turned with troubled eyes to Daphne Russell, who had also overheard.

"What's that ass Eilunedd getting at?" she muttered.

Daphne shook her head. "No idea. I don't think Peggy noticed anything; but—well, there was a lot more in Eilunedd's remarks than meets the eye. Peg's so straight herself, she'd never see it. This wants thinking about."

"O.K." Dickie agreed. "You can count me in on that."

Chapter Six

PREFECTS' MEETING

Peggy woke up next morning very early. She sat up in bed, and looked out of the window. Hurrah! The rain had gone, and the sun was shining. It looked like being a decent day. She wondered what the field would be like? Pretty sodden, no doubt. Games would be off, except for netball on the en-tout-cas courts of which there were two. Oh, well, probably they would have a good walk instead.

Having settled this in her mind, Peggy shook up her pillow and tucked it between her shoulder-blades, while she ruminated on the unexpected happenings of the night before.

"Well, there's one good thing," she thought as she lay back, arms locked behind her head, "I shouldn't have much difficulty. It isn't as if it was last term when we were new here, and we had to settle in to all sorts of strange things. And after what happened to her then, Annis Lovell will probably behave like a young arch-angel this term, and so far as I know we haven't any more queer beings unless Polly or Lala should start. With any luck we'll just have a normal, peaceful time, and probably most of our worries will consist of trying to squash the Juniors and the Middles. I'm sure I hope so!"

Her curtains moved and opened at this point, and looking round she saw Joan Sandys in pyjamas and dressing-gown. Joan slipped in, and let the curtain fall behind her.

"I thought you were awake," she said with satisfaction. "I say, Peggy, it's a gorgeous morning. Let's get dressed and go out."

59

"O.K. But be quiet or you'll wake someone, and we don't want half the dormitory tagging after us," Peggy said warningly.

Joan nodded, and slid out again, and Peggy pushed back the clothes and slipped out of bed. Twenty minutes later, she and Joan were opening a side door, and stepping out into the fresh morning air. At the same time, the seven o'clock bell pealed out.

"Rising-bell," Joan said. "I want to look at the field, Peg."

"We shan't get hockey or lax to-day if *that's* what's in your mind," Peggy said cheerfully. "It'll probably be a complete bog after yesterday's rain."

"Oh, I don't know. I expect it'll dry up all right by this afternoon," Joan returned hopefully.

"If you hope that, you're doomed to disappointment," Peggy retorted as a turn in the walk brought them to the big lawn in front. "Just look at that lawn! It's a puddle—not a lawn. You needn't be expecting the playing-field to be any better."

"Wet-blanket!"

"Well, I'm sorry, but you can't expect anything else."

"I wanted to do such a lot this afternoon if I could." Joan sighed. "There are the teams to pick as soon as possible; and the new people to try out. Peggy, what shall we do about our usual matches? I mean, we can't possibly play some of the schools we generally do. It's too far, either way."

"I suppose we'll have to let them slide for this season, and see if we can find any others to take their places as long as we're here. You're right, of course. Red Gables, for instance, couldn't be expected to do it; nor Fairleigh Grange. You'll have to go into a huddle with Miss Burn about that. I expect she's got a few ideas."

"I expect so," Joan assented. Then she changed the subject. "Look here, Peg, what have you done to upset Eilunedd Vaughn?"

"Eilunedd Vaughn?" Peggy stared. "Nothing that I know of. Why?"

Joan coloured. "Oh, just she seemed rather—rather fed up last night."

"Fed up? How do you mean? With me? But I haven't done anything *to* feed her up. There hasn't been time; and, anyhow, I scarcely spoke to her. Joan, what *are* you getting at?"

"Well," Joan began nervously, "Eilunedd seems to have some grudge against you—come to that, she seems to have it against most of us, but you in particular. No; wait, Peggy!" for that young person was trying to break in. "I wouldn't have said a word, and you know it; but Eilunedd's a queer creature. When she gets her knife into anyone that person generally has a sticky time of it. Remember when she had that row with Gwensi Howell three years ago? Everything went wrong for Gwensi that term. Her things were always turning up in Lost Property though she swore she put them away, and Beth Chester and your cousin Daisy Venables backed her up over it. And though Beth and Daisy stuck to her, she had quarrels with two or three other people she'd been fairly chummy with. No one ever said so, and I couldn't tell you *why* I think it; but I've always been certain that Eilunedd Vaughn was at the bottom of it all. Mind, I've no real reason for saying so—it's just a sort of feeling."

"Then it's the sort of feeling you'd better get rid of pronto!" Peggy retorted. "I remember the fuss there was over Gwensi's things going missing, but she always was a slapdash kind of creature, and never knew where her possessions were, half the time." She turned and faced Joan squarely. "I don't understand you, Joan. It isn't in the least like you. You've always been so fair."

Joan reddened. "I'm sorry if you feel like that, Peggy, but I can't help it. I felt I must put you on your guard. I'm not the only one to notice it, either," she added. "Dickie Christy said something about it last night, and Daphne Russell saw it too."

Peggy laughed unbelievingly. "I think you three must have come back crackers. All the same, I apologize for saying you weren't being fair, Joan. Maybe you weren't to Eilunedd; but you were being as square as you could to me. If anything happens to make me change my mind about Eilunedd, I'll apologize again in six different attitudes. And now, let's forget it. Come on and look at your lovely field!"

Joan said no more, and they went on to the field, which lay behind the house and had originally been an ordinary pasture. The hockey-field and lacrosse ground had been prepared during the previous term and the holidays, but, as Peggy had said, there was no hope of any practices that day. Even Joan had to admit it as she looked sadly at the morass the rain had made of it.

"Oh, well, it'll mean walks, then," she said. "The Middles might have netball on the courts; but that's all."

After a final look, the pair turned and walked back to the house, which was now fully roused. From some of the open windows came the sounds of people practising, and a hum of chatter greeted the two prefects as they entered by the side door.

Peggy went to seek her violin as soon as they had changed their shoes, and Joan, who was not specially musical, went upstairs to the formroom to put in a little work at her French essay. From then on, there was no time for anything but lessons and the usual school affairs, until three o'clock saw the prefects gathering in the small slip-room dedicated to their use. A long, narrow trestle-table ran down the centre of it, and there were chairs on either side, with one at the head for the Head Girl, and one at the foot for the representative of Special Sixth. Peggy entered with Daphne and Dickie, and Joan close behind. The Special Sixth girl was already there, and, of all people, it was Eilunedd! She looked up as the three Sixth Formers came in, and gave them a smile which Peggy returned.

"Hello, Eilunedd!" she said. "What does it feel like to be Special Sixth?"

"Not too bad," Eilunedd said. "What do *you* feel like being Head Girl? It's been rather a shock all round, you know. I wonder how you'll manage?"

Dickie Christy stopped short, and surveyed the speaker

with honest grey eyes. "Perfectly well," she said abruptly.
"Why on earth shouldn't she? I should say myself, Peggy
can make a better shot at it than most, seeing she's the one
of us here who has been longest in the school."

"Well, of course, that *is* an advantage, I suppose,"
Eilunedd said demurely.

"Oh, hurry up and sit down," Peggy said impatiently.
"We've heaps to do, and precious little time to do it in."

She sat down in her chair, and beckoned Dickie to her
right hand. Joan had already taken the traditional Games
prefect's seat on the left.

Dickie opened her eyes widely. One term at the school
had already taught her that she was being given the Second
Prefect's seat.

"Who says?" she demanded *sotto voce* of Peggy as she
sat down.

"Miss Annersley—this morning when she sent for me.
The rest of the jobs are ours to dish out," Peggy said.

"Miss Annersley says that Dickie Christy has been
appointed Second Prefect by the staff," Peggy began,
raising her voice. "The other posts we are to settle ourselves
as usual. These are Library—Magazine editor—Staff—
Music Staff—Stationery—Hobbies—and Special Juniors.
Frances, before we start discussing the others, Miss Annersley said I was to ask you if you would be the kids 'Special'?"

"Me?" Frances looked startled. "I'd love it of course;
but what about the others?"

"Don't you worry about us, my love," Nita Eltringham
said with a grin. "I, for one, have no ambitions that
way—get too much of it at home with all our crowd."

"Then I'd like it," Frances said.

"O.K. That's *one* thing settled, anyhow." Peggy
ticked it off on the list she had made, and was preparing
to turn to the question of Library Prefect when Eilunedd
made a diversion.

"I hope I'm not out or order," she said as she stood
up, "but I'd just like to know if the latest arrangement
is that the Head Girl suggests people for the various
posts, and we have to agree whether we do or not?"

There was a moment's silence. Then Dickie Christy and Daphne Russell both rushed in.

"What footling *rot*!" Dickie began; while Daphne, with equal heat, cried; "Didn't you hear: or are you deaf?" with supreme sarcasm. "Peggy said the Head had suggested Frances for the job."

"Oh? Well, I just wanted to know," Eilunedd replied meekly.

"Well, you *do* know," Peggy told her shortly. "As for the other posts, you'd better all make lists and let me have them. Mollie, you're nearest the cupboard. Make a long arm and reach out some paper, will you?"

Mollie complied, and when they were all settled with a sheet of paper before them, Peggy said; "Well, the posts are Library—Magazine—Staff—Music Staff—and don't forget that it's no use appointing anyone to *that* job who doesn't take music!—Stationery, and Hobbies. Joan, Dickie, Frances, and I are all out of the running as we have our own jobs fixed already."

"And Eilunedd too, I suppose?" Judy Rose mentioned sweetly. "She's here as Special Sixth representative, and they don't have any special job, do they?"

"Not up to date," Peggy replied; and Eilunedd flushed up.

The girls set to work to make their lists, and when they were finished, Peggy told off Dickie and Frances as tellers, while Joan made hay while the sun shone, and laid before the Head Girl a list of people to captain the various school teams.

"We've finished," Dickie announced. "One or two of them were very close; but I think this lot is correct. However, the lists are here if anyone would like to check up on us."

"Anyone want to?" Peggy asked, looking round the table; but even Eilunedd felt that it was unnecessary.

The reason for her behaviour was not far to seek if they had but known. She had expected to be in Upper Sixth this term, and had fully expected to be there as Head Girl. Her father, however, had felt that at nearly eighteen it was time she was beginning to concentrate on one thing, as she had no wish for college. She was not a particularly clever girl, and had shown no real bent in any direction. Therefore he had settled that she should take a secretarial course, dropping all maths and science, and going on with English, French, and German, with Spanish for a third language. Eilunedd had not minded the idea until she had reached school and learned that as a result she was to be in Special Sixth, and would therefore not be eligible for the post of Head Girl. She was a jealous girl, inclined to brood over fancied wrongs, and this was an outsize one. She had no special grudge against Peggy Bettany until it was announced that that young lady was to have the post she had expected herself. Then the sullen anger which lay in her was stirred, and she was out to make things as awkward for the innocent Peggy as she could.

To make matters worse, her own close friends had left unexpectedly at the end of the last term, and though the rest of her new form were friendly enough, she had no particular chum now, so out of school-hours she was going to be at rather a loose end. Most unfairly, Eilunedd blamed the whole thing on Peggy, and vowed within herself that Peggy Bettany should find that being Head Girl this year was not going to be all jam.

As no one raised any objections, Peggy read out the list. "Library, Barbara Henschell; Magazine, Daphne Russell; Staff, Judy Rose; Music Staff, Mollie Carew—got a pain, Moll?" for that young woman had clutched her head with a loud groan.

"I should think so! Aches all over! Miss Cochrane *doesn't* love me, and now I've got to take that wretched exam she'll love me less and less as the term goes on. *Why* couldn't you pitch on someone else?" she wailed.

"There didn't seem to *be* anyone else," Dickie said. "Peggy is booked anyhow, and Nina is the only other one who takes music. We really are a most unmusical crowd!"

"Gwen and Hester and Barbara Smith all take music," Eilunedd said.

"Yes; but they aren't prefects," Dickie retorted.

Mollie sat up. "Oh, I'll do it! If I die as a result during the term, kindly remember that sweet peas are my favourite flowers, with pansies second. Go on reading, Peggy, and let the rest know the worst."

Peggy chuckled. "It only leaves Nina for Stationery and Nita for Hobbies. Is that all right, everyone?"

"You know," Eilunedd said, "I don't want to seem to be grumbling, but it does seem queer to me that Speical Sixth are always left out. After all, I can't see any reason for it. Most of us have been prefects already, and are therefore experienced."

"Yes," Joan reminded her, "but then as a rule we have a good Upper Sixth who have also been prefects previously, and they take over where the others left off."

"Exactly!" Eilunedd spoke impressively. "And that's just where I think the Heads could easily have made a change in the ordinary arrangements, and allowed members of Special Sixth a chance of prefectships this year. It was an excellent opportunity to break away. After all, it's never good for anyone to get into a rut, is it?"

"Why don't you go and see either Bill or the Abbess on the subject?" Nina said sweetly. "I'm sure they would be pleased to hear your views on it. Probably they hadn't thought of it, and your ideas would be *quite* fresh to them!"

"Oh, come off it, both of you!" Dickie said crossly. "Bill and the Abbess both know jolly well what they're about, and they wouldn't thank anyone—not any of us, at least—for going and criticizing their doings. Is it likely?"

Peggy, who had been too startled by the turn things were taking to interfere, now stood up. "That's enough, all of you! Nita and Nina, are you willing to take over those jobs? And the rest of you? We all know Mollie's views; what about you others?"

"It's O.K. by me," Judy replied. "It just means seeing

that the Staff get their elevenses, and so on, isn't it? I can manage that."

"And I can manage Library, I think." Barbara, a great reader, looked pleased. "Anyway, it's the job I'd have chosen if I'd have been asked. Thanks awfully for electing me, everyone."

Daphne Russell chuckled. "I can't say mine's exactly the job I'd have chosen, but I'll do my best. When should I ask to have this term's contributions in, Peggy?"

"Oh, give them three weeks or so," Peggy said easily. "I should put up a notice saying that all contributions to the magazine must be handed to the editor by three weeks on Saturday. That'll give *them* time to produce something, and *you* time to go over it, and ask for further things if you have to chuck out too much. Don't forget that when you've made your final selection the lot has to go to Miss But— Oh, *crumpets*! I'd forgotten: we haven't Miss Burnett any more! Does anyone know which mistress has taken her place?"

"Won't it be the new one—what's her name? Anyone know?" Nina looked round the table, but they all shook their heads.

Nita had a brilliant idea. "Auntie Jo—I mean," in some confusion, "*Mrs. Maynard* is coming for *our* history, and she's a real live authoress. What's the matter with having her for magazine mistress?"

They all applauded this idea loudly—even Eilunedd.

"You really are a brain, Nita!" Dickie remarked. Then her face fell. "I say! Isn't it the *Heads* who choose the magazine mistress?"

"It is," Peggy agreed, "and in that case, the job's done. You don't suppose Bill and the Abbess are such owls that they'll let a chance like that slide, do you? I'll tell you what, Daph: you go and grab one of them, and ask who you should show the magazine stuff to when you've got it as Miss Burnett has left. You might even," she added, "hint that it should be Auntie Jo. You know; 'Who will be magazine mistress now, Miss Wilson? Will Mrs. Maynard take that over with our history?' That sort of thing. Bill will be on it like a knife. She's not *lacking*!"

"Oh, thank you, Peggy," said Miss Wilson's voice at that moment, and the girls turned, horror-stricken, to see her standing in the doorway. "I suppose you haven't all gone deaf," she continued, advancing into the room. "I've knocked three times, and I couldn't wait any longer, as Nita Eltringham is wanted on the phone. Run along Nita, dear."

Nita jumped up, her face paling, and hurried off, and the younger member of the Head partnership gave the girls a brilliant smile. "I don't think I can usually be accused of being inquisitive," she remarked, "but I *should* like to know what it is that drew forth Peggy's stately compliment just now."

In much confusion, Peggy stammered out: "It was just that we had suddenly remembered Miss Burnett has left, so we haven't a magazine mistress now, and Nita suggested that Auntie Jo would be the very one to take it on. I—I said you and Miss Annersley would see that all right, and—and——" she ran down at this point.

"Especially," Miss Wilson agreed, "as Jo herself was editress of *The Chaletian* for some years—in fact she was the first editress. Of course we had thought of it, and Miss Annersley will tackle her on that point when she comes over for her first lessons with you next week. Well, if that's all, I must go. I'm a busy woman." She smiled at them again, and departed to leave them to recover themselves as best they could.

"Eilunedd, you're nearest the door!" Joan cried. "Why on earth didn't you hear Bill knocking?"

For once, Eilunedd had nothing to say, and Peggy, making an effort, brought the meeting to order. "It might have been worse. But we'd better make less noise in future. Let's finish this up. Our time is nearly run out."

"There's only Nina to ask, and she isn't here," Barbara pointed out. "I don't suppose she'll mind, and she's the cleverest of us all at handcrafts and that sort of thing.

I say," she added in a changed tone, "I hope there's nothing wrong at her home."

"If it had been that, they wouldn't have asked for her," Peggy replied sensibly. "One of the Heads would have been asked to tell her."

Nita herself returned at that moment, and from her beaming face they guessed that it was all right.

"Only Uncle Nigel," she said. "He's bringing Aunt Rosamund on the yacht for a week-end to stay with Mr. Bellever on Brandon Mawr, so they'll be coming to see us—Blossom and Judy and me—on Saturday, and they wanted to be sure we wouldn't be away. Well, have we finished?" She suddenly began to giggle. "Whatever did Bill say to you folk after I left? Peggy was holding forth about her, and she must have heard *something*! What happened?"

The rest broke into peals of laughter at the memory.

"Oh, she just asked what she had done to deserve Peggy's stately compliment," Judy bubbled. "Peg went all colours of the rainbow, and began some sort of explanation, but Bill just said of course Mrs. Maynard would be asked to take over the Mag. Anyhow, she'd been the first editress of it. I suppose that would be in Tirol?" she added, turning to Peggy.

"Oh yes. *The Chaletian* was a going concern when I first went to school," Peggy agreed. "Auntie Jo ran it for quite a time. Then—I don't know—oh yes: it was handed over to Eustacia Benson."

"Who was she?" Eilunedd demanded. "I've never heard of her."

"Good heavens! Not heard of Stacie Benson!" Nita exclaimed. "Why, she's the E. Benson who's been doing translations of some Greek stuff—don't ask me what, for I don't remember!—that have made a tremendous stir in the world. I've heard Dad talking about them, and he said they were wizard!"

Eilunedd opened her eyes. "Was that a pupil here once?" she cried. "I've heard *my* father on the subject, and he said they were the most scholarly works of the kind he's ever seen. But I thought it was a man did them. You don't mean to say it was just a girl?"

"Well, she's not exactly a girl now," Peggy said, tugging at a curl that had come loose from her slide. "She must be quite thirty. But she used to be at this school."

The little cuckoo clock on the mantelpiece suddenly cuckooed the hour, and they awoke to the fact that their time was up.

"Four o'clock," Peggy said. "Well, we've got all the jobs fixed. That's one good thing. Oh, before we all go, I've got a message from the Head. Will we please try to put a stop to the appalling amount of slang that some of the kids are using. The slang-fines box wasn't here last term, but it's been brought now, and we are all to see that people who use too much of certain words are duly fined. I don't somehow think that the Middles and Juniors are going to love us very dearly for the next few weeks," she added with a grin, as she picked up her pen, and left the room to prepare for tea.

Chapter Seven

SETTLING IN

While Peggy was trying to adjust herself to her new position, the two new girls she had brought to school with her were also making adjustments. Nor were they finding it very easy. Peggy had taken it for granted that Polly would probably be with Bride in Upper Fifth, seeing that they were much the same age; therefore she had asked her sister to give a hand where she could. As for Lala, at nearly fourteen she ought to be in Upper Fourth along with

Peggy's young cousin, Sybil Russell, and Sybil's chums, Blossom Willoughby and Susannah Wills. She had handed Lala over to Sybil as soon as she could, with strict injunctions to give an eye to her until she knew where she was, and Sybil had agreed cheerfully.

Unluckily, it hadn't worked out like that at all. Years of slacking over lessons had left Polly and Lala a long way behind even the worst of the two forms Peggy had chosen for them in her own mind. When they had finished their entrance papers, the results were that Polly found herself in Lower Fifth, and Lala was sent to Lower Fourth, so neither Bride nor Sybil could be much use. They had been placed in dormitories with quite other girls, too; and Peggy was so much occupied with her work and out-of-school activities, that for the first few days she had little time for more than a hasty, "How're things going? Everything all right?" when she ran across either of them.

Lala got on better than Polly. She was an easy-going girl, taking life pretty much as it came. By the end of the week, she had resigned herself to the fact that she must be with people younger than herself for the most part, unless she chose to work. She had plenty of brains, as the school was soon to find out, but she was lazy, and little inclined to use them unless someone prodded her on. Until they had taken her measure, the staff were lenient with her, and she thankfully settled down to doing just as much work as would pass muster, and giving herself up to enjoyment of a whole crowd of girls, and all their various ploys.

Lower Fifth, in which Polly finally found herself, boasted only nineteen girls. The form prefect was a small, pixy-like girl, named Betsy Lucy, who was a good nine months younger than Polly, but who, nevertheless, soon proved that she had plenty of brains under the smooth golden-brown thatch that crowned her head. Her special friend, Primula Venables, was also a clever girl, though somewhat frail health had kept her back hitherto. This promising pair set a standard for hard work in their form, and though people like Clem Barrass, Nicole la Touche, and Pat

Collins had no real love of lessons, as a form they worked well and steadily.

Polly's horror at finding herself among a crowd who, taken by and large, worked in school whatever they might do out of lessons, may be easily imagined.

The first morning after the new girls were finally placed, they had algebra, followed by history. Then came French and geography, and the amount of preparation set filled the Lady Acetylene Lampe with dismay. Five examples in simultaneous equations; a written question on the Hundred Years' War; an exercise on the uses of Pouvoir, *and* a climate map of South America stunned her.

"When have we to do all this?" she asked Betsy Lucy at the end of morning school.

"In prep, of course," Betsy replied, staring in some astonishment.

"And when's that?"

Betsy scanned the time-table which was conveniently near at hand. "Three to four this afternoon, and five to half-past six this evening."

"Do you actually mean that after all the work we have to do during the day we've got to start again after tea?" Polly sounded stunned. "When do we get any time for play?"

Clem Barrass, who was near, chuckled. "We've an hour for games this afternoon. And we've all the time we want after six-thirty."

"But that's no time at all." Polly spoke very definitely. "And as for the games, that's just another sort of lesson, isn't it?"

Lower Fifth stared at the new girl, bewildered by this novel outlook. It had never occurred to any of them to look on their games as "lessons."

Primula spoke up in her shy, soft voice. "You don't call games lessons exactly."

"I do, when it's things that you have with a mistress," Polly assured her. "Don't we ever get any time off to do as we like?"

"Of course we do—Saturday afternoon, unless there's

72

a match on, and Sunday, too, so long as we don't go tearing about and making nuisances of ourselves. We go to church, of course; but that's all. Someone reads aloud to the kids, but we are supposed to be able to amuse ourselves without that," Betsy said.

Polly said no more, and as Lower Fifth wanted to discuss the new history mistress, the subject dropped. All the same, she pondered on it with some disgust. She and Lala had been so accustomed to running wild, that she felt pent in by all this. Even the rousing game of hockey which started scarcely helped, since naturally she had never played before.

Preparation was a revelation to her as well. The girls sat quietly at their desks, most of them working hard.

Polly opened her new Godfrey and Simmonds, and set down the first equation in her queer, niggling script. She had done some algebra, and knew the rules fairly well, but up till this, she had never troubled to care whether her work was right or not. Now she began to work the sum out, and arrived at an answer that any sensible person would have seen could hardly be right, seeing that she made x equal five times as much as the whole thing. However, it was finished, and she tackled the next. This, for some odd reason, she quickly worked to the right answer; the other three were either wildly wrong, or else done so carelessly that it was clear that she had not bothered much with them.

Algebra ended, she opened her Heath and looked at the exercise. "He could not come because the weather was bad." How on earth did you say that in French? What *was* the French for 'could,' anyhow? She hunted through her vocabulary, and naturally was unable to find it. That settled it! No one had any right to give them an exercise with words that weren't in the vocab! Polly gave it up, and proceeded to write: "Il ne——pas venir parceque le temps etait mauvais."

The effect on Mlle de Lachenais when she corrected the sentences next day can only be described as hair-raising!

The bell rang for the end of preparation by the time

Polly had written her last word. She heaved a loud sigh of relief; but it was quickly succeeded by one of disgust as she remembered what still had to be done.

Tea followed, and then they all went upstairs to change into the brown velvet frocks which were daily evening wear during the Christmas and Easter terms. Polly, in her cubicle, pulled on her frock, dabbed at her head with a brush, and was then preparing to leave the dormitory, when its head, Primrose Day, appeared from between her curtains. She cast a horrified glance at the gollywog mop and exclaimed: "Oh, Polly, you can't go down looking like that!"

Polly drew her thick eyebrows together in a scowl.

"Why not?" she demanded. "I've changed, and I'm clean. What's wrong?"

"Your hair! You look like a shock-headed Peter! Go back and give it a good brushing, do!" Primrose urged.

"Oh, rats! I'll do nothing of the sort!"

Polly had, of course, no idea of the authority wielded by the head of a dormitory, or she would scarcely have replied like this. Half a dozen heads peered round the curtains at her words, and Tom Gay, also a member of it, appeared, fully dressed and immaculately tidy, to say: "Here, I say, you can't speak to Primrose like that! 'Tisn't the done thing. And anyhow," she added, after a look at the untidy mop, "if you *don't* do as she says, the first staff that meets you will send you back to do it, and that'll mean losing an order mark into the bargain."

Having flung down the gauntlet, Polly was not prepared to withdraw. "Well, let it!" she retorted. "I'm not going to be bossed by a girl of my own age—or any other girl either, for that matter," she added.

"Do as you please," she said curtly. "It's up to you."

It wasn't so easy for Primrose, though. She was a conscientious girl, and she knew that if Polly went down looking as she did at the moment, someone would say something. Polly, however, gave her no chance to do anything more. With another scowl she tramped along the

74

corridor, wishing from the bottom of her heart that she had never so much as *heard* of the Chalet School. She was suddenly brought up short by a tall, very dark lady who seemed thoroughly at home there.

"Hello!" said this character. "You're one of the new girls, aren't you? Now let me see: who are you?"

"Polly Winterton," the owner of the name growled.

"Of course! I should have guessed it. O.K. Well, I'm Peggy Bettany's aunt, Mrs. Maynard. I've heard about you." Jo stopped, and looked with pleasant interest at the tall, lanky redhead before her. "I say, Polly, someone's been jolly careless in not telling you about the rules here. Haven't they told you that you've got to be tidy—not a hair out of place—when it comes to the evening? I *should* know," she added with a grin which held something of the same schoolboy quality as Tom's. "Heaven's knows I got into enough rows for hair all over the shop when I was your age. As for when I was *growing* my hair, well, my head was like a porcupine with hairpins. Still, that won't interest you fearfully. What *does* matter to you is what Matey will say if she catches you looking such a mess. Come on back to your cubey, and let's see if I can't do something about it for you."

Polly's first impulse was to tell Mrs. Maynard to mind her own business. Luckily she opened her lips to say it, only to close them again. Something in the quizzical look Jo was giving her made her crimson, and then turn meekly round and go with that lady back to the dormitory, where Primrose and the rest were just coming out. A yell of delight went up, bringing Matron on the scene in short order.

"*Girls*! What is the meaning of this noise?" she demanded.

"Me," Jo said meekly, coming from behind the door, where she had slipped when her quick ears caught the sound of Matron's brisk step.

"You seem to have changed a good many of the rooms round this term, Matron."

Matron nodded. "We did it during the holidays,"

she assented. "You must remember that last term we just had to fit in as best we could, for everything had to be done in such a rush at the last. However, we've arranged things quite nicely now. Suppose you come along to my room for a few minutes and let these girls go downstairs before they are all late for preparation."

"O.K.," Jo agreed. "I'll see you later, Polly, and meantime you'd better buck up and finish or you really will be late." She gave the girl a meaning look, and Polly, who had felt Matron's eyes going to her untidy head with a look there was no mistaking, slipped off to her cubicle, and presently appeared in her formroom, looking as tidy as Tom herself. Primrose and Co. exchanged glances, but no one said anything as the new girl went to her locker to collect her books.

Whether it was the little excitement that helped her, no one could say, but Polly set to work on her history with considerably more interest than she had shown over her afternoon's work. The drawing of her map occupied her for some time. When it came to filling in the various areas of climate, however, she was well and truly stumped. She fidgeted with her coloured pencil, and cast anxious looks at the others working steadily round her. Most of them had finished the map, and were hard at French or algebra. Only Nella Ozanne, sucking her pencils till her mouth was ringed round with green, was busy with it, and Nella sat three or four desks away. Polly heaved a deep sigh. Betsy Lucy glanced up from the French she was copying out from the rough work she had done, and met the new girl's eyes with their look of bewilderment. She got up and came quietly to her.

"Anything wrong?" she asked in a low tone. Then, as her eyes fell on the outline, she gasped: "I say! Did you really *draw* that? Bill *will* feel she's got hold of a genius at long last!"

"Oh no, she won't!" Polly snapped. "I can't think of a thing to put into it."

Betsy thought for a moment. "You'd better take it next door to Upper Fourth," she said finally. "Dickie Christy's

76

on duty there, and she'll give you a leg-up. Go on, Polly; it's quite all right. We're allowed to ask for help. Dickie won't *do* it for you, but she'll tell you how to go about it."

Polly got to her feet, picked up the map, and departed for Upper Fourth, where she found the same atmosphere of concentration. Dickie Christy was at the mistress's table, busy with a sticky piece of Livy, but she glanced up as the new girl came in, map in hand.

"Yes? What is it?" she asked pleasantly.

"I've got rather tied up over this," Polly explained unwillingly, "and Betsy said I'd better bring it to you. We haven't anyone with us."

Dickie opened her eyes. "Well, you're Fifth Form, aren't you?" she said. "You folk shouldn't need looking after like this lot."

Polly put the map before her and Dickie looked at it with admiration.

"Jolly good map!" she observed. "Memory work? Right! Now what have you to do with it?"

"Mark in the climates," Polly told her tersely.

"Oh! Well, don't you know them?"

"Not awfully well."

"I see. You aren't allowed to use your atlas, of course? O.K. Now listen to me. What sort of climate do you expect to find at the equator? No; don't tell me. Find your equator, and mark that off. Remember that mountain ranges will make a difference. Now, will the south be hot or cold? Think that out, and mark it. Then try to remember where your great plains are, and remember the prevailing winds blowing towards the central part. If they're wet, you'll get seasonal rains. If you have a part with high mountains between it and the coast, just think that you won't get much in the shape of rain unless you have other bodies of water near it or on it. Be sure to give a key at the bottom of your map so that Miss Wilson can see what you are getting at. That all O.K.? Right! Then off you go and get cracking. You'll soon get accustomed to working things out. It's mainly a matter of practice.

Polly saw that Dickie had finished with her, so she said

"Thank you!" and left the room. However, thanks to Dickie's hints, she was able to put *something* into her map, even though some of her ideas proved distinctly odd. Thanks to Jo's intervention upstairs, and the help Dickie had given her, she began to feel that just perhaps life at the Chalet School might not be quite so bad as she had feared at first.

Chapter Eight

JOEY'S NEWS

"Ready Sybil? O.K. Come on, Bride and Maeve. We'll have to step out or we'll miss the ferry, and then we'll be done."

"What about Len and Con," Sybil Russel demanded as she pulled on a glove. "Aren't they coming too?"

"Not to-day. Auntie Jo said she wanted us bigger ones by ourselves, and you know what those two are like." Peggy suddenly looked puzzled. "All the same, it's queer. Auntie Jo said she had news for us. I wonder what it is? Evidently something she doesn't want the kids to know—or not yet."

Bride Bettany, swinging along between her younger sister and her cousin, opened her eyes. "At that rate, should we take young Maeve?"

A howl broke from Maeve at this horrible idea. "Of course you should! Auntie Jo *asked* me. Anyhow, I'm not going back now. What a nasty sister you are, Bride!"

Peggy laughed. "Oh it's all right as Auntie Jo asked her. Scoot on and open the gate, Maeve,"

"I expect she's heard from Mummy or Dad when they're

coming back," Sybil said happily. "Some time next month, isn't it? That's what they said when they went.

Peggy was recalling her aunt's words of a few evenings ago. Auntie Jo had said the news was good in some ways, she supposed, but she hadn't seemed very pleased about it. Could it possibly be that the Russells and Margot Maynard were not returning as soon as they had hoped? That would be a drop for everyone, including Sybil. The Head Girl glanced at the unconscious face of her cousin, and hoped that it was not that.

Bride had glanced at her watch. "I say! We'd better scram!" she exclaimed. "We haven't any too much time."

"Take Maeve's other hand, then," Peggy said, grabbing the one nearest her. "Now then, Maeve, get cracking!"

Helter-skelter they went down the road, Bride and Peggy somewhat hampered by Maeve, whose ten-year-old legs were much shorter than theirs. Sybil raced ahead to hold up the ferry if necessary; but when they reached the little landing-stage, it was all right. Peggy tossed down the fare as she pushed her small sister before her, and they arrived on board, breathless and panting, but safely there.

The crossing took twenty minutes, so they had cooled down and regained their breath by the time she drew up at the quayside at Carnbach, the small Welsh port which was their nearest land. Jo Maynard was there to welcome them, Michael, the youngest of the Maynards, in his pram, while Charles and Stephen, the other two boys, stood one on each side until their cousins were safely on shore. Then they ran, and for a few minutes there was a babel of chatter.

"How Michael is growing!" Peggy said when at last Jo insisted that they must get home. "He won't be a baby much longer."

"I know," his mother said. "He's almost as big for his age as Steve was, and he was always enormous."

"He's a big boy now," Peggy said, with a look after the young man who was trotting ahead with his hand in Sybil's, while his tongue was going nineteen to the dozen. "He's a lot more like seven than five. How does he like his school, or hasn't it begun yet?"

"Not till next Thursday," Jo said. She raised her voice. "Hi, you people! Not so fast! I've got to call in here for the potatoes."

"Can't I take them home, Mamma?" Stephen suggested. "You and Peggy could come along behind."

Jo laughed. "No reason why not. Very well; you show the way. Peggy, hang on to the pram for me, and mind Michael doesn't try to fall out. I shan't be a minute." She vanished into the shop, and Peggy was left to wait outside, and wonder to herself just why her aunt had secured her for a private interview like this. It wasn't like Aunt Jo not to want to be the first to show off her new home. If she hadn't wanted a talk, she would have told Stephen to wait.

Jo returned before she had managed to work out any answer to the problem. She brought a big bag made of hessian and full of potatoes with her, and Peggy sprang to help her. Michael had been watching his opportunity. With a chuckle of triumph, he stood up as far as his harness would let him, and then bumped down again, starting the pram on a run down the sloping pavement. Jo shrieked and dropped her bag, the potatoes rolling in all directions, while Peggy grabbed at the handles of the pram just in time to stop it rolling over the kerb and into the road, down which a bus was coming. Even so, it took the pair of them all their time to keep it from going over, and by the time they had it righted and on the pavement again, half a dozen small children had appeared from nowhere, and were gathering the potatoes with guttural Welsh exclamations.

"You naughty boy!" Jo exclaimed as she set her son straight. "If you do that again, I'll have to tighten your harness,"

"Mam-mam!" Michael said sweetly, lifting eyes like forget-me-nots to her face.

"I mean it," she told him. "A nice mess there'd have been if Peggy hadn't been so quick!" She turned to thank the children who had collected the last potato, and were handing the bag to her. I say, thanks so much. Wait a moment." She felt under the coverlet of the pram, and produced a bag. "Can you share these? Good!"

The children took the bag, with shyly uttered, "Diolch mawr's" before they scampered off, and Jo, having slipped the handles of her bag over the pram handles, began to set off up the street.

"Well, after that excitement, let's get back to everyday life," she remarked. "How's school going, Peg?"

"All right, so far," Peggy replied. "We haven't been back long enough for anything much to happen, though. I say, Auntie Jo, wasn't that your sweet ration?"

"Yes; but I couldn't thank them in Welsh, and I had to do something about it, hadn't I? I should have warned you what Michael is like. He's the wickedest of all my family with the exception of Margot. In fact, those two are a pair!"

"Probably Margot will have improved in that direction when she comes home next month," Peggy said, feeling her way a little.

Her aunt gave her a look. "All innocence! No, Peg, my lamb! I don't expect to see my bad youngest daughter for a good deal longer than that—worse luck!"

Peggy turned a startled face to her. "Not for some months!" she exclaimed. "What's happened, then? No one's ill, are they?" she added.

"Not so far as I know," her aunt replied. "No; it's nothing like that. Uncle Jem is anxious to join some group or other who are experimenting with a new drug that they hope will help with T.B. in bones. It's a great honour to be invited, and naturally he wants to accept. He *can* be spared from the San for such a reason, and so it's been decided that they stay in Canada until next May or June."

"But—but—that means they'll be away more than a year!" Peggy cried in dismay.

"Auntie Madge says in her letter that she's been torn in two. She misses David and Sybil terribly, even though she has half her family with her. But she also says that the visit is doing both Josette and Margot so much good that she feels she must stay there for their sakes, even if she didn't want to leave Uncle Jem. So there we are!—Turn up here: this is our road, and Cartref is at the far end."

They had left the lane for a quiet road with houses standing in their own gardens at either side. The road was a long one, and as they went up, Peggy could see that where the houses ended, there was a meadow, leading to a little wood.

"I say," Peggy began, when they were half-way up the road, "what about Sybs? The kid's been looking forward to having Auntie and Uncle and the other two back for weeks now."

"It means eight months more at the very least. I'm simply dreading having to tell her. Len and Con will make fuss enough when they hear that they've got to do without their third for a while longer. Sybs will be infinitely worse."

"Why doesn't Auntie Madge come home with the kids for a month or so?" Peggy demanded. "After all, they could fly."

"I was on the trans-Atlantic phone to your aunt. She won't hear of it. Says she isn't going to risk the kids' precious necks in any plane, never to speak of her own. She *did* suggest that it would be quite a good scheme, though, If *I* did it. However, I wasn't having any, any more than she. I've the boys and your Uncle Jack to think of; and we've just moved in here. As it is, I'll have to go every once in so often to see what's happening at Plas Gwyn. Anna's there to-day, by the way. She wanted some pots and pans we'd left in a cupboard in the part that's all right. I've got Rosa from the Round House, though. Here we are. How d'you like it?"

Peggy stopped at the gate, and looked up the short circular drive at the house. "It's a lot smaller than Plas Gwyn," she said.

"We'll just have to put up with being a bit cramped for the next few months. It'll make us appreciate Plas Gwyn when we go back," Jo said philosophically.

All the same, when she and the others had been escorted all over the house, Peggy thought privately that her beloved aunt was going to miss the roominess of her old Queen

Anne house far more than she said. Cartref was a double-fronted house, with the dining-room at one side of the door, and the drawing-room at the other. They were fair-sized rooms, and very pleasant, facing the south, and getting plenty of sun. The kitchen lay behind the dining-room with a serving-hatch between. Behind the drawing-room was a small room where Dr. Maynard had put such items from his home study as he felt he *must* have with him. Above this floor was the main bedroom floor, and Jo had turned the room over the dining-room into a nursery and play-room, keeping the other large one for herself and her husband. The room behind theirs was the boys' bedroom, mainly because there was a door between the two. The one on the other side of the passage was for the girls. The bath-room was over the front door, and must have been origin-ally a dressingroom. Upstairs were four attics and a box-room. One front attic had been handed over to Anna, Jo's great mainstay; and her cousin Rosa, who had begun as Lady Russell's nurse in Tirol, and remained with the family ever since, would share it with her. The other front attic had two little beds in it, and Jo told Sybil that she and her cousin Primula must share this.

"As for a guestroom," the mistress of the house said resignedly, "there just isn't room for one. Robin and Daisy have the other two attics when they are here, and if we want visitors, one will have to double up with the other. Thank heaven it's only for the next few months!"

"I know what you'll miss most," said Bride solemnly.

"Oh? What's that?" her aunt demanded with interest.

"The *cupboards*! Plas Gwyn is such a house for cupboards and closets, and there's awfully few here. However will you keep the place tidy with nowhere to shove things?"

"You cheeky brat! Are you implying that I *can't* be tidy without glory-holes?" Jo demanded indignantly.

"We-ell, you aren't a Miss Prissy Prim, are you?" Bride said with a chuckle. "Where are you going to write your books?"

"In the alcove in the drawing-room. Didn't you notice that curtained-off place? I've got my desk and a chair there, and I'll have to manage with that. Well, that's everything, I think. Suppose you go to the bathroom and wash your hands before we go down and look at the garden?"

"The garden? I thought you had only that bit in front," Peggy exclaimed.

"If that had been all, I don't think we *could* have managed It isn't though. Wash, and then come on, and I'll show you." She shooed them firmly into the bathroom, and then went to the nursery where Rosa, having taken the small boys' coats and caps off and changed their shoes, had left them to play together while she saw to tea. Jo told them to be good boys until Mamma came for them, and then went down to the drawing-room, where Peggy was already waiting.

"When are you telling Sybs, Auntie Jo?" that young lady asked.

"Not till after tea if I can help it. I'll send the rest of you upstairs with the boys. Then if she is badly upset, I'll keep her with me till Monday morning." Jo pulled aside the curtains at the alcove, rummaged among the papers in a drawer of her desk, and then produced a letter which she tossed to her eldest niece. "There you are. You can see what Auntie Madge says, but keep it to yourself. Here come the others, so stand by, Peg, and keep Sybs off the question of when her people are returning if you can."

Peggy nodded, stuffing the letter into her blazer pocket.

Jo left the alcove just as the crowd thronged into the room "Come on!" she said. "I'll show you the garden. This way!"

She led the way through the kitchen and the tiny scullery off the kitchen, where there was a door opening into the yard. They crossed the yard, and went through another door between the wash-house and the coal-house as Jo explained briefly. Once they were through this door, they found themselves in a back lane which they also crossed, and came to a door in the high wall that ran down the side. Jo produced a key, and opened the door, and the girls found themselves looking into a pretty garden which ran back to a little orchard. Beyond, as their hostess informed them, was a kitchen garden, the first part being given up to a lawn with borders filled at present with dahlias, chrysanthemums, and late roses, and crazypaved walks. A little pool was in the centre, with a tiny fountain, and stretched out in the sun was Jo's beloved St. Bernard, Rufus, who had been hers ever since, as a Middle of thirteen, she had saved the tiny puppy of six weeks from drowning. He lifted his head as his mistress came into the garden, and then got to his feet with a 'Woof!' of welcome before he trotted over to her.

"Had enough, old man?" she said, kneeling down to hug him. "See who's here!"

Rufus had known Sybil and Peggy and Bride from their babyhood, and he went from one to the other to greet them. He was a very old dog now, but great care and his own hardy breed had, so the vet said, given him every chance of living for at least two or three years longer. He was very much one of the family, and the girls petted him delightedly before they followed Jo round the whole of the little estate. When they had seen everything, they went back to the house, accompanied by Rufus. The sun was begining to slant to the west, and he was much too precious to be left outside when evening came with its dews.

Tea went off very well. Jo filled cups, and pressed buns and cakes on her guests, and chatted merrily about school and school affairs, anxious to keep Sybil off the question of her parents' return. But at last no one could eat or drink anything more, even the small boys having had enough. Mrs. Maynard sent Bride and Maeve upstairs with them to stay there until Rosa arrived to begin putting them to bed. Then she turned to Peggy, who was watching her with sympathetic eyes.

"Like to go to the study and ring up the Quadrant, Peg?" she asked.

Peggy jumped up. "Oh, Auntie Jo, may I? That would be super!"

Peggy sped from the room, and Sybil watched her go with a face full of longing. I wish I could ring Mother up," she said.

Sybil went over to the big settee drawn across the open french window at the side, and sat down. "It'll be lovely when they do come," she said wistfully. "You don't know how I've missed them all!"

"It's been just as bad for David," Jo reminded her.

Sybil thought. "In a way, I suppose it has," she admitted. "But boys are different, Auntie Jo. And then David's been away from home whole terms for years now. He's in the Rugger team, and the debating society, and he's working jolly hard this year—he told me so. He wants to be a doctor like Dad, you see,"

"Yes, Sybs, I agree it's a little diferent for him. All the same, I expect he's missed them pretty badly." She paused there, looking anxiously at her lovely niece.

Sybil was far and away the pick of the second generation. With eyes of brilliant sapphire blue, she had dark coppery curls framing a face with delicate features and exquisite tinting. There had been a time when her beauty had brought her into grave danger of becoming unbearably conceited, but a bad shock some years before had ended that. Her own wilfulness had caused a serious accident to her next sister, Josette, at that time the family baby, They had nearly lost Josette, and Sybil would never forget how greatly she had been to blame. The child had never really been robust since, and this was one reason why her parents had accepted the Canadian invitation to an important medical conference. Jo felt that Sybil would hark back to that dreadful time when she heard the news that was awaiting her.

"Do you know exactly when they're coming?" Sybil asked. "No one has said anything to me, and I don't think they have to David."

Now for it! Jo braced herself to meet what was to come.

"I know something," she said quietly. "I had a long letter from your mother this week, and she told me that they aren't coming in October as they expected. Your father has been invited to take part in a very important affair. It's a great honour, Sybs, and one he would like to accept, so— they are staying for the present."

"What? Not coming back soon? Then—when? *How* soon, Auntie?"

"Well, not this year," Jo said.

"Not this *year*!" Sybil repeated incredulously. "But—what about Christmas? What's going to happen to David and me if we can't go home?" Then as the truth of it began to dawn: "Auntie Jo! There's nothing *wrong*, is there? Josette—she's all *right*, isn't she?"

"Fit as a fiddle," Jo made haste to assure her. "No, Sybs; so far as I know they're all in bounding health. But Canada is doing them all so much good—especially Josette, and—and Margot, that they are staying till this business of your father's is ended."

Sybil drew a long breath of relief. "Thank goodness! I—I was afraid——"

She could get no further, and her aunt caught her in a hug. "Oh, my poor lamb, don't worry about that! Your mother says that Josette is blooming now, and no one would ever think she'd had an illness in her life. Ailie is growing enormously, too and is as sturdy as can be. Even my Margot is much stronger, and you are old enough now, Sybs, to know that we've had a lot of worry with her."

"I know," Sybil said slowly. "She's had such a lot of bronchitis. And then she was so ill with that bad throat."

"Yes, poor little pet! But from what your mother says, she's going to be like Josette—pounds and *pounds* stronger for this trip. As for Christmas, the whole family—including all of us *and* Rufus—are going to the Quadrant. So you won't have to worry about that." She put the girl from her and looked at her anxiously. "Sybs, you *will* try not to fret over this, won't you? I know it's dreadfully hard on you and David——"

"It's hard on you too," Sybil interrupted.

Jo stared at her in surprise. "It is, of course; but then I'm so glad that Margot is growing strong, that I can put up with it. Besides," she added, "I'm a good deal older than you, Sybil, and I've learnt to wait for my good things. It's a hard lesson, but if we learn it properly, it does help to make life easier for us."

Sybil nodded. "I want Mother and Father just *awfully*," she said, "but I'm like you Auntie,—so glad that Josette is getting really fit after all this time, that I'll just have to put up with it and not grouse. After all," she added with a sigh, "it was my fault in the beginning."

"Josette's illness certainly was," Jo agreed. "I was desperately sorry for you, Sybs, during that time—sorrier for you than anyone else, even your mother. It was hard for her to see Josette suffer, and know that there was a chance that she mightn't live; or even if she did, she might never be well again. But it was even worse in one way for you. Madge had nothing to blame herself for. She's always been a wonderful mother, and she'd done everything she could to help you all. If anything dreadful had happened, you would have known it was your fault. Now, my lamb, you can forget all that. It's finished. Josette is going to be as sturdy as any of you. So promise me not to think of it any more."

Sybil shook her red head. "I can't do that. I don't think I'll ever forget it. It was a *ghastly* time. But I'll promise you not to be miserable about it again."

Peggy returned just then, very much refreshed by a brief chat with her mother, and Jo, after a glance at the clock, stood up. "I must go and see to the boys. Peggy, you people ought to be getting ready to go back. The ferry leaves in half an hour, and we're a long way from the landing. I'll send the others down, and when you're ready I'll be with you."

"O.K.," Peggy said; but she followed her aunt as she left the room. "Auntie, I haven't been able to read Auntie Madge's letter."

"That's all right. Take it with you and let me have it on Monday. I'm coming across then to begin your history lessons," Jo told her.

"Wizard!" Peggy said appreciatively. "Thanks, Auntie."

"And Peg keep an eye on Sybs, will you? She's taken the news much better than I expected; but she may fret over it in private."

"I'll do what I can," Peggy agreed meekly; but, as she

went to seek her hat and gloves, she gave herself a little impatient shake.

"Oh dear! I never knew such a term as this! I came back to school prepared to be a junior prefect and then I'm landed for Head Girl. I'm supposed to give an eye to Polly and Lala, and see that they settle down quietly. Now I have Sybs to add to everything. What a life! It seems to me that the older you grow the worse it becomes. Oh, and I'm not so sure that Joan was wrong in what she said about that awful ass Eilunedd. Anyhow, there was clearly something behind all her chat at the prefects' meeting. Heavens! At this rate I shall be *white* by the end of term!"

At this point, Bride and Maeve came sliding down the bannisters, and Peggy had to give up her gloomy thoughts and help her small sister to get ready to go back to school. Jo came down a few minutes later, and rejoiced all their hearts by informing them that she was going to get out the car and run them to the landing-stage so that there should be no danger of their missing the ferry.

"It's been great fun," Bride said as she kissed her aunt good-bye. "When can we come again?"

"Not for a few weeks, anyhow," Jo told her cheerfully. "Buck up, Bride. You'll see me on Monday, I expect." Then she whispered to the girl: "Be good to Sybs. Peg will explain why when you're alone."

Then they had to scuttle, for the ferry whistle was blowing, and the men were waiting to hoist the gangway.

Chapter Nine

NEWS FROM CANADA

Peggy was so busy once they were back at school, that it was not until the next afternoon that she was able to tackle the letter from Canada. However, the day broke dull and foggy, and though they were able to go to morning service at the village church, by the time they came out the fog was thickening, and when dinner was over, it was clear that there could be no walk that afternoon. The girls retired to their own common-rooms with books, puzzles, and paint-boxes. Miss Norman and Miss Edwards took their own small folk off to be read to; and Hilary Burn good-naturedly volunteered to help Miss Stephens with the Juniors. The rest were expected to need no supervision; but if they did, Miss Slater, the senior maths mistress, and Mlle Berné were sitting in the staff-room. Therefore the prefects felt free to amuse themselves as they chose. Peggy escaped to her cubicle. There, she pulled the curtains down, settled herself in her wicker-chair, and opened the many sheets of Lady Russell's letter.

"My dearest Jo," she read. "First of all for my report. Everyone is in bouncing health, I'm very glad to say. Margot has just left me to go for a walk with Jem and our two, and I never saw such a collection of blooming cheeks as the three of them have produced. Even Ailie has developed red roses, and she was always naturally paler than any of the others. I've had to outfit the lot afresh, for they've not only grown much taller—Josette grows like a scarlet runner!—but they're literally bursting at the seams! Unless Len and Con have kept pace with Margot, she's going to leave them well behind."

Peggy turned the page with a chuckle. Len and Con had both taken to growing lately, and their mother had groaned loudly to her over the fact that they must have completely new outfits for next term as she and Anna had let down or out every hem and seam to its fullest extent already.

"Just the same," she murmured to herself, "Auntie Madge isn't in any hurry to get her real news. I expect she knew what Auntie Jo would have to say on the subject. I wonder if she's let Mummy know?"

She settled down to the next page.

"Who do you think we met last week—Friday to be exact?" the letter went on. "Corney Flower, of all people.

She looks very fit and well, and has got rid of her glasses at last. Also, she showed me a very lavish diamond ring, and invited me to be her matron-of-honour at the end of October? I suggested it might be as well to have someone nearer her own age, but she laughed and said she'd rather have me. And anyhow, the three little girls *must* be her bridesmaids. By the way, she rather rudely told me that *of course* she'd have asked you if you'd been available, but she guessed you were too much tied up with your long family to be able to spare even a fortnight to come to Boston, which is where they have settled down, and where the wedding will be. I agreed!

"All the same, Joey, it's quite an idea. Couldn't you leave the boys and Jack to Anna for a brief space and fly. We'd love to have you and I know you'd love Canada. It's time you had a holiday from your family, Jo. I'll not forget what Jack said about you in a hurry when he wrote at the beginning of the summer holidays. My dear girl, what *were* you thinking about to let yourself get into such a state? I very nearly told Jem that if he *must* stay, he could stay alone, as you evidently needed your elder sister to put down a firm and heavy foot on some of your activities! So what about it, Jo?"

"Gosh, how awful!" Peggy sat bolt upright in her chair. "What on earth would the kids do if Auntie Jo departed, even for a few weeks?"

"Departed where?" demanded Bride's voice. "Can I come in, Peg?"

"Yes; come in," Peggy replied. Then, as Bride appeared, she waved the sheets of the letter. "Come on and hear what Auntie Madge has to say. Auntie Jo gave it to me to read, and I'm sure she wouldn't mind you having a dekko at it. Auntie says all the kids are bursting out of their clothes and she'd had to get them new things all round. And do you remember Corney Flower, Bride? You were only a wee thing when she left, of course."

Bride laughed as she squatted on the floor. "Of course I remember her. Anyway, she's almost as much a legend in the school as Auntie Jo is. What about her? Has Auntie Madge run into her?"

"And how! Corney's going to be married and she wants Auntie Madge to be her matron-of-honour unless Auntie Jo can be coaxed to fly to Boston for the wedding." Peggy sat back and eyed her sister expectantly.

"But she couldn't possibly," Bride protested. "It's bad enough having Auntie Madge out of the country. Auntie Jo can't go off as well! When is the wedding, anyhow?"

"End of October."

"Then, of course, she can't! It's the Trips's birthday on Bonfire Night. Even if she flew, she mightn't be able to get back in time. Supposing there was bad weather and all planes grounded? A sweet time we'd have with young Len and Con!"

"I think you're right there," Peggy agreed. "Well, that's as far as I've got. Do you want to read it for yourself, or shall I go on?"

"Oh, go on. I can see the first part later on."

Peggy took up the second sheet. "Here goes! 'You know, Jo, I don't quite know what you are going to say, but the fact is we shan't be back in October as we expected. One thing after another has cropped up, and to crown everything, Jem has been invited to stay at the James M. Mather Sanatorium where they're going to try out some new drug this autumn which is hoped to be a great help if not a complete cure to T.B. bones. *He* gives it some grand Latin name, of course; but bones will do for me. They've been experimenting with it for some years now; and they're going to use it on men in this place, now they've found it really does do the trick with animals— apes, I believe. It's a tremendous compliment to be asked, and he's yearning to agree, so I don't quite see how I can refuse: do you?

" 'Again, it does seem a pity to *be* here, and not stay to see the Canadian winter. Everyone tells me I really ought not to miss it, and what is more to the point, Dr. Merriman, who has the girls under his care, says that while Ailie is as sturdy as they come, the bracing cold would be the right thing for both Josette and Margot. His last report was that Josette has finally recovered all she lost during those awful years and Margot's tendency to chest trouble is greatly improved. If they could have the winter months here in the dry cold, he thinks that, humanly speaking, we need not worry about them any further.

" 'All this being so, and as we have been offered an extended lease of our present house, we have decided to take advantage of it. And so—and oh, Joey, don't be too furious with us!—we shall stay our year out.' " Peggy laid down the sheet and picked up the next.

"Poor Auntie Madge!" Bride said unexpectedly.

"Why?"

"Well, I expect Auntie Jo went up in the air over the phone to her, even though she's agreed to it. You know what she can be like."

"Ye-es," Peggy spoke slowly. "I expect she had quite a lot to say. All the same, Auntie Jo's a reasonable person, and once she'd got the worst off her chest, she'd be all right. If Canada is really going to mean the end of worry about Margot, both she and Uncle Jack would give in. They've had some pretty tough times with that kid."

Bride nodded, looking grave. "It's weird that kid should always have been so groggy when the other two are so fit. She really is the only one of Auntie Jo's crowd that's been much worry that way. Even young Charles hasn't been the anxiety to them that Margot has."

"I asked Mummy about that when they first went away," Peggy said. "She said it often happened with twins—that one of them wasn't quite as strong as the other, I mean—and it was likely to be even more so with triplets. All the same," she added, "it hasn't worked that way with our lot. Rix and I have always been fit; and I don't believe Maeve and Maurice have had a day in bed in their lives—except for sins."

Bride laughed. "They are a wicked pair, aren't they? As for you and Rix, you're fit enough now, but you surely remember all the fuss there used to be when you so much as sniffed? Auntie Jo explained to me that when we had measles years ago when Jackie was a baby, you were awfully ill with it, and they had to be careful with you for a while."

"I'd forgotten all about that. Still, that was measles. Well, shall I go on?"

Peggy turned to her letter again, and read on.

" 'I'm afraid I'll have to ask you to break the news to David and Sybil, and I do hope they'll both understand. I don't think you'll have much trouble with David. He's a very sensible fellow, and a placid creature too. I'm much more afraid of how Sybs may take it. I'm writing to them on Sunday, so they'll hear from me next week. In the meantime, Jo, be a dear and tell Sybs, at any rate. I don't want her to build on seeing us at the end of October, and then be let down with a bang. You know how she works herself up about things. And write to David for me, won't you? I'd do it myself, but, thanks to having to see to new outfits, I simply haven't had time for letters, and I do want you and Dick to know as soon as possible. Do you think perhaps he or Jack could run down to Winchester to see David and tell him?

" 'Tell Len and Con that we are making a collection of various things to bring home to them. There'll be parcels for Christmas and their birthday too. By the way, thank you for the lovely doll's furniture for Ailie; she proposes to write to you herself—she can print quite nicely now— but it won't be much of a letter. Jem gave her a pair of stilts, if you please! All three have them now, and they go all over the place on them. We're buying little sleds for them for Christmas. Most of the children here seem to have them, so our three would feel out of it if they didn't; though what use they'll be once we get back to England, I don't know.

" 'You know, Joey, though I'm simply aching at times to come home,' "—Peggy laid down the sheet and took up the next—" 'part of me is simply longing to see a *real* winter with dry, powdery snow, and thick, *skateable* ice

94

again. Not that I can see myself doing much skating for the present. Help is almost non-existent; and with three scaramouches to look after as well as all the housework, I shan't get much time for fun of that kind. Jem will see to it when he has time. If not, I don't doubt that their schoolfriends will manage for them. I've had to let them all three be very much more independent than they would have been at home. The children here learn to look out for themselves pretty early.

" 'À propos of your last letter, of course they're not Americanized. As if I'd let them! I admit they've picked up several Canadian expressions, but they have *not* developed a twang! How horrid of you, Jo!' "

Bride emitted a chuckle. "How like Auntie Jo! I'll bet she pulled Auntie Madge's leg well and truly about it. Is it nearly done, Peg? I'm not exactly warm."

"Pull my eiderdown round you, then," Peggy advised. "There's not a lot more." She went on with her reading.

" 'If you really want to know, both Jem and I have been most particular about that. It hasn't been easy, either. Margot seems to be able to pick up anything like that— their French mistress at school congratulated me on her French accent—and Ailie isn't far behind her. Josette has been the least trouble that way of the three.

" 'We are taking them to a very good photographer's here to have photos done to send home for Christmas. What's the matter with you doing the same by the rest of them, and sending the photos out to us? I'm asking Mollie to see to it with her crowd too.

" 'We do miss you so. I do, anyhow. Jem, being full up with his various conferences etc. hasn't the time. Margot is getting over her fits of weeping for you and her sisters. We had one or two bad times with her after the novelty of everything had worn off. At first she was too excited about the new life; but since then, she has been a very sorrowful little mortal once or twice. I didn't tell you before, because I knew how you would worry. However, it's more or less at an end now, and she seems quite resigned to staying. As she says, there'll be all the more to tell when she does see you all.

" 'Well, Joey, I seem to have written you a volume. Think over Corney's suggestion, won't you? I'd love to see you. If you can't come for the wedding, what about coming at the end of November and staying for a while. But then you wouldn't want to be away for Christmas. Well, try for the spring, then. Why not come for Easter, and bring the children with you? Then we could all come home together; for I can assure you I don't intend to stay here any longer than the end of May or the beginning of June. Explain to Hilda and Nell, and I'm sure they'll agree to giving the girls leave. That means my Sybil as well, of course. We daren't ask for David just when he seems to have settled down to steady work at last. But Sybs, bless her heart, will never set the Thames on fire, and means to go in for art needlework and designing in any case, so half a term out of school wouldn't hurt her.

" 'Give my love to everyone, including all your own small fry, and the Bettany girls. What is this weird story of yours about Peggy being Head Girl? I thought she was only Upper Fifth last year. Don't you mean head of the junior prefects? It's a new idea, of course, but quite a sound one, and would be an excellent grounding for being the actual Head Girl of the school next year.

" 'I've just remembered that that will be her last year. It doesn't seem possible! It's only the other day that you were mooing all over the place because *you* had been made Head Girl. Peggy was a baby of four or so then. I can scarcely believe that she's old enough to be thinking about leaving school altogether. But do write by return and tell me just what you do mean about this Head Girl business. I'm quite bewildered. Next, you'll be telling me that Sybs is a prefect. I warn you I shan't believe *that*!

" 'I had a letter from Robin last week. She seems to be very happy in her work, and doing very well. All the same, it's not quite the life I envisaged for her. Well, she's only—how old? *Twenty-two*! Oh dear! Why will you all insist on growing up? Not that *you've* ever done much at that. Please don't try, either.' "

Bride giggled. "It all seems to be awfully on Auntie Madge's mind! Does she really think we're all going to stay mere kids all our lives?"

Peggy laid the last sheet down for a moment. She looked thoughtful. "In a way, I can see what she's driving at," she confessed. "You know I had a letter from Aunt Frieda the other day? Well, she told me that Louis will come to school in England with Maurice next year, and I got quite a shock. He was such a tiny boy—only four, when we last saw him. I counted up, and he's *seven*! Gerard must be five; and the baby will be two. She'll be trotting about all over."

Fifteen-year-old Bride didn't see it. "Well, you'd expect that," she said bluntly. "I'll tell you what, though, Peg. The thing that has given me the biggest shock is realizing that you are old enough and so on to be Head Girl of the school. I don't wonder Auntie Madge simply doesn't believe it yet. But I thought Auntie Jo was going to phone her when she knew?"

"Yes, she said she would; but it didn't come off. When she got home that night Uncle Jack was there to tell her just how much more must be done to Plas Gwyn than they'd ever thought, and she forgot all about the school. If you come to that, it was a big shock for *me*. However, I'd better finish this, and then you must trot off downstairs."

Bride nodded, pulled the eiderdown closer round her, and Peggy took up her page again.

" 'Jem had to go to New York a fortnight ago, and stayed with Bernhilda and Kurt von Eschenau. They are doing very well, and he says their family is delightful. Stefan is exactly like his grandfather, Herr Mensch, and Hilda is Bernie over again. Louise is Kurt's image, and Francis is a neat mixture of both, with Kurt's colouring and Bernie's features. As for the baby, Jem says it's too soon to say, but he fancies she'll be another Hilda. They've called her Marie Gisela, and she's to be Mariel for short. Bernie is very thrilled to have five, and Jem says that

Hilda and Louise are too funny with her. I suppose ten and nine are at an age to be motherly, though Sybs was never that way inclined even with Ailie.

" 'Well, that's all my news this time. I'm hoping to go and see Bernie and Co. myself some time before we leave Canada, but it won't be just yet, though I may try to squeeze it in if I go to Boston. After that I mean to take things quietly. It's all been such a rush this year, what with tearing off to Canada like that, and having two removals since, not to speak of our trip to Vancouver in August. I no sooner seem to settle down than I've to uproot again, and after our peaceful years at the Round House I find it too exciting to be quite pleasant. Goodbye for the moment, Joey, and think over what I said about coming over in the spring with the children and my Sybil. Much love. Madge.' "

"That all?" Bride asked as Peggy began to straighten the sheets.

"Quite enough, don't you think? It's a lot more than I could manage. Shove that eiderdown back on the bed, Bride, and then pack off to the common-room. It must be nearly tea-time."

Bride stood up and stretched herself. "Ow! I've got pins and needles in my feet sitting like that. O.K., Pegs; I'm going." She went to the window to look out. "I say! The fog seems to be thinning. I shouldn't be surprised if it was all gone by to-morrow, and we got our games after all."

Peggy, having folded the letter and returned it to its envelope, came to the window to look out.

"It's thinning all right," she said, "but I don't think you folk will get your games for all that."

"What d'you mean?"

"Well—just listen!"

The pair stood silent for a moment. Then Bride shook herself. "I don't hear a thing—or nothing out of the ordinary."

"There!" Peggy held up her hand. "Hear that queer moaning sound?"

Bride nodded, her eyes widening. "Yes, I do now. What on earth is it? Wind?"

Peggy nodded in her turn. "Wind, my lamb, and wind that means mischief. We've heard it often enough at home in the winter. That's a nice storm wind that's coming. We've never seen a storm on this coast yet, but I should imagine it won't be any gentler than ours when it happens. Unless I miss my guess, we're going to have a snorter."

Bride shivered. "Beastly! I loathe storms at sea." A sudden idea struck her. "I say, if it really does come and is as bad as you think, what price Auntie Jo and your lessons?"

"They won't come off—unless the Sound is sheltered enough for it not to matter. It may be. We'll just have to wait and see. There's the bell for tea, and your hair looks as if you'd been dragged through a hedge backwards. Scram, or someone will send you flying from table to make yourself fit to be seen." As she spoke, Peggy cast a hasty glance at herself in the mirror of her bureau.

"All right; I'm going. It's well to be folks with curls. *They* never have to worry about untidy hair," Bride grumbled as she departed to comb her mouse-brown locks into something that would pass muster with Matron, just in case that lady happened to see her.

Peggy stayed only to drop her aunt's letter into a drawer, then she went off to join the rest of the clan for their Sunday privilege of tea by themselves in the prefects' room, and no more was said about the letter from Canada.

Chapter Ten

STORM WIND

The storm Peggy had prophesied blew up during the night. Most of the girls were too soundly asleep to hear the wind rising; but they woke in the morning to find the air full of noises that were anything but sweet. The wind was blowing great guns, and mingled with its blasts came the crash of mighty waves as they swept down to dash themselves to a flying rain of spume against the granite cliffs. The Sixth, emerging from the house to make a dash across the big stable-yard to the science lab and geography room for the first part of the morning, found heaped-up masses of yellowish foam lying on the cobbles, and even in that sheltered space had to hold on to head scarves as they scuttled over into shelter.

"Phew! What a gale!" Nina gasped as she turned to shut the door behind her. "Hi, Dickie! Give me a hand here, will you? It's more than I can manage."

"Rats!" retorted Dickie, nevertheless coming to the rescue. "It's not so bad as all that. There you are!"

The door was safely shut, and the girls trooped into the various rooms. Not all the Sixth took science, and those who did not had an extra geography lesson, so that they were kept together in the outbuildings for the morning, since the second part was occupied by their art class, and the art room, being an army hut, led out of the old stables which had been converted for science, geography, and domestic science. The gymnasium was also in this part of the grounds, and as the two lots parted, they could hear Miss Burn briskly issuing commands to Lower Fourth, who had the first lesson on Mondays.

Miss Wilson was waiting in the science lab, and Miss Stephens came racing across to the geography room just after her class had settled itself, quite pleased to find that the mistress had not yet put in an appearance.

Peggy, Barbara Henschell, Gwen Evans, Daphne Russell, Nina Williams, Judy Carew, and Hester Layng were obliged to postpone the chat they had promised themselves, and give their attention to a lesson on the effect of climate and relief on distribution of population. Mlle Lachenais came to them for the second period, and as she was free for the first, she was waiting at the door when Miss Stephens left them, so all talk had to be left until break, which they had in the 'Dommy Sci' kitchen with Lower Fifth and Upper Fourth, who had just come from Gym.

Dickie Christy, who was on break duty that day, briskly poured out the cocoa for those who wanted it, while the rest solaced themselves with glasses of milk. When her job was done, she grabbed her own cocoa and biscuits, and joined the select little group of prefects which had retreated to the far end of the kitchen.

"Listen to that wind!" Peggy said. "It seems to be blowing harder than ever. Dick, do you think the ferry will be running to-day?"

Dickie shook her head. "Not very likely—though it isn't often it shuts down for wind," she added. "Just the same, I don't think they would risk it a day like this. The gale's still rising, and it looks like growing a lot worse yet. Just look at those clouds! If you ask me, we're in for a good old-fashioned storm, and it won't calm down for a day or two. Your Aunt Jo won't have a chance of coming over this end of the week, Peg, my lamb, if that's what you're thinking."

"Well, she can't phone," Nina said cheerfully. "I heard Miss Dene say that the wires must be down, for the phone was dead. So what?"

"Shut up with slang, Nina," Joan Sandys retorted. "Blossom Willoughby and Co. can hear, and they don't need any encouragement in that line."

Nina sighed. "It's hard lines to have to talk like a Jane Austen heroine," she said. "I'll do my best though."

"Oh no, you don't!" Peggy was down on her. "None of your 'vastly' and 'monstrous', and all the rest of it."

Nina chuckled. "I doubt if I could keep it up very long. O.K., Joan; I really will try to remember. It doesn't look too well for a prefect to have to patronize the fines box."

No one noticed that Miss Blossom suddenly looked thoughtful; nor that she grabbed the arm of Sybil Russell, and edged the pair of them a little nearer the prefects. In any case, the elder girls had dropped the subject, and were chatting about the storm.

"What shall we do during history period this afternoon?" Frances Coleman asked.

"Wait and see if anyone hands anything out, I should think," Dickie said. "If they don't, I suppose we'd better read on. We've a fearful lot of ground to cover for the exam. I could do with an extra hour here and there quite nicely myself. Listen! Isn't that the bell? We'd better go. I'll just see what the kids do next. Someone fix me up with painting-water and a drawing-board, please." She turned to demand of Gwen Parry, the Upper Fourth prefect, what their next lesson was, while the rest of her compeers went off to the art room to prepare for their lesson.

Upper Fourth were due for geography, and Upper Fifth had already departed for chemistry, so Dickie saw to the Middles settling down in readiness for Miss Stephens, and then joined the others, to find that Herr Laubach, the art master, had blandly presented them with sprays of spindleberry and the command to work out a design for dress material from it.

The lesson lasted two hours, from eleven until one, as a general rule, but half-way through, the inter-house telephone bell rang, and presently Blossom Willoughby appeared with a message from Miss Annersley to say that, as the storm seemed to be getting worse, she would like the girls to come over to Big House at once. A tile had crashed down from one of the smaller outhouses, and she had seen its descent and taken alarm. It was true that the girls had a very short distance to run, but tiles and slates might just as easily crash down into the stable-yard as the garden, and the Head was taking no risks.

Herr Laubach himself had noticed the steady rising of the wind rather uneasily, so he made no bones about the matter. He bade the girls pack up as fast as possible, and hurry back to the house.

"I will come and give you a brief talk about design for the remainder of the time," he said, glancing at the huge turnip watch he carried in his waistcoat pocket. "Make haste, please, young ladies."

The girls jumped up, and began to put their work away. The others had already left the place when at last the Sixth, with their scarves tied tightly over their heads, were ready to leave the outside classrooms. Herr Laubach brought up their rear, taking the keys to lock up, as Miss Wilson, Frau Meiders, and Miss Stevens had already departed.

He held open the door, and the girls, taking advantage of a brief lull, began to race across the cobbles to the side-door of the house. Peggy, as Head Girl, and Dickie, as second prefect, were the last to go. Peggy put up her hand to hold her scarf down, prepared for the dash, when through a sudden blast of wind an unmistakable sound rang out.

"Rockets!" she cried. "There's a ship in distress somewhere!"

"The Mermaidens!" Dickie exclaimed. "Oh, poor souls! They won't have a chance in a storm like this if it is! The sea must be raging now!"

Herr Laubach gave her a push. "Make haste to the house," he ordered. "Peggy, please tell Fräulein Annersley that I have gone to see if I can be of any assistance." Cramming his cap down over his brows, he turned and left them, hurrying out of the yard by the small door cut in the great outer doors.

The two girls had nothing to do but obey, and this is certainly what they should have done. Dickie had turned round to lock up, since the master had not stopped to do it, when a second rocket sounded.

"Come on, Peg!" she said. "I'm going to see what it is. We might be able to give a hand somewhere."

Peggy said afterwards that she thought the wind must have got into her brain, for she grabbed at Dickie's outstretched hand, and together the pair scuttled across the yard and slipped through the door which Herr Laubach had left open, and which was banging with the wind. Dickie drew it close behind them, and they set off down the shrubbery to reach the orchard, which was a short cut to the lane that led to the cliffs. They had a certain amount of protection here; but once they were in the lane, they met the full force of the rising wind, and had to stop frequently and turn their backs to it in order to get their breath. It was after ten minutes or so of this that sanity returned, to Peggy, at any rate.

"Dickie!" she shouted. "We can't go on in this! Miss Annersley and Bill will be dancing as it is. Come on; we must go back!"

The wind whipped the words out of her mouth, and Dickie, her jaw set stubbornly, only realized that she was speaking. Despairing of making her chum hear, Peggy pointed back the way they had come.

"We—must—go—back!" she yelled, at the full pitch of her lungs.

Dickie caught the drift of her remark this time, and shook her head. "I'm—going—to see!" she bawled.

They had reached a turn in the lane, and Peggy knew that a hundred yards farther on it would swing round to the open cliff-top, and she guessed that, bad as the wind was here, it would be infinitely worse there. She grabbed Dickie's arm, digging her heels into a muddy rut, and held on.

"Dick! We can't!" she bellowed, as Dickie struggled to free herself. "We couldn't stand!"

Dickie made no reply, but fought fiercely to get free. Peggy slipped in the mud, and fell, dragging Dickie on top of her, and thus knocking the remaining breath out of the pair of them.

By the time they had got to their feet, Dickie's common sense had returned to her; and as if to make the state of things quite clear to the silly pair, there came a fresh gust of wind, accompanied by a dreadful creaking and groaning, and Dickie, with a wild yell, swung Peggy back against the hedge just as an elm tree at the curve slowly heeled over, falling across the lane, and most effectually blocking any passage to the cliffs.

The two girls whitened as they stood, barely safe, and saw what the force of the storm had done. Peggy shook, as her vivid imagination saw the pair of them under the tree, crushed by the weight of the trunk, maimed—perhaps killed. Dickie was spared this, but their narrow escape had completely sobered her. She put her arm round the trembling Peggy, holding her fast.

"All right?" she yelled, putting her mouth close to Peggy's ear.

The Head Girl nodded. It was all she was capable of doing at the moment, and Dickie realized that they must get back at once. She only hoped that Peggy wouldn't faint before they got there. Still holding the other girl firmly, she turned round, and began to pull her back along the lane. Once they were away from the bend, it was easier, for they had a certain amount of protection from the hedge, and in any case, the wind was behind them. They reached the orchard, and crossed it, though Peggy felt each step an effort. Then they were in the shrubbery, where shelter was better, and the Head Girl's strong will was coming to her aid.

Not even yet were they out of the wood, however. They had just reached the far end when there came a fresh blast, and with a crash a slate from the roof cascaded over to smash on the paved walk a scant foot beyond them. Both yelled, and Dickie cast an anxious look at her friend; but this second shock had helped to eliminate the effect of the first, and Peggy looked more like herself as she hurried with Dickie to the side-door, where they burst in to fall into the arms of a grim-looking Miss Wilson, clad in burberry and hood, just coming in search of them.

She pulled them in, and shut the door before she said anything. Even as she opened her lips, the rockets came again, this time from father away, and a wail broke from Dickie.

"That's Brandon Mawr! There won't be a chance! Not with those awful cliffs! Oh, it's too ghastly!" After which, to her everlasting shame whenever she thought of it, she burst into tears.

"*Dickie!*" Peggy gasped in dismay, as she flung an arm round the weeping Dickie. She looked up at Miss Wilson. "I'm awfully sorry, Miss Wilson. Herr Laubach heard the first rocket at the Mermaidens go off and he rushed off to see if he could be any help. Then—I don't know— Dickie and I—well, we—we——" Peggy ran down under Miss Wilson's grim expression, and went scarlet.

"I think you had better come to the study," that lady said curtly. "Bring Delicia along, please, Margaret."

The use of their full Christian names brought home to Peggy as nothing else could have done the enormity of their conduct. She felt serious qualms as she piloted Dickie along the empty corridors to the study where Miss Annersley was awaiting them. Peggy stole one glance at her face, and then, big girl as she was, shook in her shoes. She had never, in all her almost seventeen years, seen the Head look like that.

Miss Annersley looked at them steadily. Dickie had given up all attempts at self-control and was howling even as her small sister Gay might have done. Peggy was still very white, but she had got a grip on herself now. As she said later, *some*one had to keep sane!

"Sit down, girls," the Head said gravely. "Delicia, please stop crying like that. It won't mend matters now."

Peggy's head went up. She faced the angry Head fearlessly. "It isn't because of what we did that Dickie's crying," she said. "Just as we came in, we heard rockets going off from over Brandon Mawr way. If any ship's gone on the rocks *there*——" She stopped as she remembered the great granite cliffs, falling sheer down to the sea, and suddenly felt sick. Miss Wilson had been watching her, and she quickly shoved a chair under the girl's shaky knees. "Sit down!" she said, as she came to take Dickie from her friend. "Put your head down and don't lift it until I tell you."

Thankfully, Peggy collapsed on to the chair and did as she was told, while the younger partner of the Heads put poor Dickie into a corner of the settee, and left her to pull herself together.

Peggy felt all right in a moment, but Miss Wilson kept her bent down until she was certain that all danger of faintness was over.

When at last she told Peggy to sit up, that young woman felt as if she must suffer from a rush of blood to the head. She raised herself quickly and sat back in her chair, her hands folded in her lap, her blue eyes steadily fixed on Miss Annersley.

"You feel better?" The Head's voice was very grave.

"Yes, thank you, Miss Annersley," Peggy replied.

"Then I should like an explanation, if you please."

Dickie had pulled herself together. She stumbled to her feet and came over to where Peggy was sitting. "It was my fault, really," she said, ending with a sudden catch in her breath. "Peggy did say we must come back; but if it hadn't been for the tree falling, I don't think I would —that, and Peggy trying to haul me back."

"Tree falling?" Miss Annersley spoke quickly. "What do you mean?"

Between them, the two girls managed to give a fairly full account of their adventures, and the two Heads shuddered inwardly as they listened. The pair had escaped death by a hairbreadth. So much was plain. Not that either of the mistresses gave a sign of what they felt, and Peggy, glancing first at one impassive face and then the other, began to dread what was coming.

"Fortunately," Miss Annersley said, when they had finished and she had kept silence long enough to ram home her extreme disapproval of their goings-on, "no one but

107

ourselves knows what you did. I should like to point out, Margaret, that *you* are Head Girl, and you, Delicia, are second prefect. I should also like you to tell me if you think your conduct at all fitting."

Silence.

"I am waiting for an answer," Miss Annersley reminded them when the silence seemed to her to have lasted long enough. "*Do* you think you have behaved as a Head Girl and second prefect ought?"

"N-no," Peggy faltered.

"And you, Delicia? What have you to say for yourself?"

Dickie flushed. "I know it was mad, but—well, when I heard those rockets, I knew what it meant, and somehow nothing else seemed to matter," she said. "I'm very sorry, Miss Annersley. And please, don't be angry with Peggy. She did try to make me come back."

"Yes; but not at first," Peggy reminded her quickly. "I forgot everything, too, just at first."

There came a loud pealing at the front door bell, then Olwen, one of the maids, burst into the room. "Oh, if you pleess, Mam," she gasped, her words tumbling over each other as she became more and more Welsh in her excitement, "if you pleess, it iss Mistress Maynard——"

At this point, she was put to one side, and a drowned rat of a creature came swiftly into the study. "Hilda—Nell! Thank goodness we're safely here!" Joey cried. "We've been shipwrecked; but, thank God, no lives were lost! They decided to run the ferry across as the Sound *is* sheltered, but she got into the current—and we tossed so—well, *wallowed* comes nearer the mark—that if you'll believe it, I was very nearly seasick! Anyhow, Captain Morris managed to get us into that queer little bay beside the landing, and then we grounded, and she just heeled slowly over on to her side. Mercifully, she acted as a sort of breakwater, so we were able to get ashore, and Commander Christy was down there helping, so he ran me to the gates in his car. And here I am!" At which point Joey suddenly looked round and saw her niece and Dickie Christy. "Mercy on us!" she ejaculated.

"Is it a judgment? What have you two been up to?"

Peggy was suddenly galvanized to her feet. She leapt at her aunt regardless of her dripping state, and flung her arms round her.

"Oh, Auntie Jo!" she cried, "if Auntie Madge ever hears of this, she'll come home by the first plane. You might have been drowned!"

"That's enough," said Miss Wilson, coming to from the stunned amazement Joey's appearance had thrown her into. Peggy, you and Dickie run off and make yourselves fit to be seen. The bell will be going for Mittagessen in a minute or two, and you look a couple of sights. Off with you!"

The pair made haste to vanish, and when they had gone, Miss Annersley proceeded to deal with her ex-pupil.

"*Why* you should have been so mad as to try to cross to-day, Jo, only you yourself know. I hope you've had a lesson for once. You won't get back this night, let me tell you, for I won't take the responsibility, even if they can get the ferry righted and run her across."

Jo made a face at her. "Keep calm, my love! keep calm! I haven't the least intention of trying it on. Once of a shipwreck in a day is enough for me. I told Anna I probably should stay over to-night, so no one will worry if I don't turn up."

"Come and have a bath and change," Miss Wilson said. "Do you want to catch a cold?"

"Sea-water doesn't give you cold. All the same," she added, as she followed the two Heads from the room, "I must admit I've been more comfortable in my life."

They all laughed at this, and then Joey was firmly escorted to a boiling hot bath, and afterwards given dry clothes. This was followed by a cosy little lunch in the study, and when the bell rang for afternoon school, she sailed into the Sixth Form room looking her usual self, and proceeded to make hay of anyone's hopes of having extra time for reading.

Chapter Eleven

CURE FOR A REBEL

It took three days for the gale to blow itself out, and by that time Joey had nearly succeeded in making herself an object of dislike to the Sixths. She studied their time-tables with concentration, and thereafter, whenever they hoped to settle down to a free period, they were frustrated, for Mrs. Maynard would appear, smiling blandly, and announcing that they might as well make use of the time for a little history. As the Sixth Forms all looked forward to free periods as a means to getting on with work that was behind time, this upset their plans considerably. Peggy blew up in private on one occasion, but her aunt remained sweetly adamant.

"Sorry, and all that," she said airily, when she had heard all the girl had to say, "but if this weather is a fair sample of the sort of thing we can expect here in the winter, I'm making hay while the sun shines. I've had one experience of shipwreck, and it's going to be the only one in my life if I've any say in the matter. For the future when we have a storm, I'm staying at home. Therefore, my lamb, I propose to make the most of my time here now, just in case. You folk have an appalling amount to put in before any of you are ready for your exams. Unless I see reasonable hope that you'll do me credit I'll refuse to have you entered for history, at any rate."

"*Oh!*" Peggy cried in exasperation, "you really are the—the outside of enough, Auntie Jo!"

"Is that the latest way of calling anyone the limit?" Jo asked with interest.

Peggy gave it up after that, and fortunately for all

concerned, the storm ended that night, and Jo was able to return to Carnbach and her small boys, while the Sixth Form people thankfully went back to the normal time-table and their free periods.

The next day, the rain came, and once more the girls were prisoners, for it thrashed down with a violence that would have drenched through the stoutest raincoat in less than a quarter of an hour.

"I'm sick of this," Vanna Ozanne said, as she gazed pensively out of the window on the Friday morning.

Her twin came to join her at the window. "We haven't a lawn any more," she said mournfully. "It's a young lake."

"Oh, well"; Vanna retorted. "I suppose this won't go on for ever. What are we doing after Prep to-night, anyone?"

"Hobbies as usual, I expect." Primrose Day from Upper Fifth had entered the common-room in time to hear this. "With luck I ought to finish the last corner of my tea-cloth. How's your furniture going, Nella?"

Nella, the elder of the twins, sighed. "Not at all. I've run out of wood, and until we can get across to the mainland I can't do a thing at it. Matey said she'd give me some remnants for sheets and curtains and things like that, so I suppose I'd better see her about it after tea. Tom's making a most super house this time for the Sale and we want to fit it up with all sorts of extras, so if I can't do one thing I must do another. It'll take us all our time to get the things finished by Easter. Audrey, how are the carpets going?"

"One finished, and one nearly finished—but it's awfully finnicky work," Audrey Simpson told her. "Still, I think it'll be worth it."

"I'll say it will. I never saw anything daintier than the one you showed me last week."

"From all I hear it's going to be a wizard affair," Elfie Woodward, also of Upper Fifth, remarked. "What sort of a competition are we going to fix up for it this time? You remember Bill said last Easter that we must get another idea. We've made people guess the name of the house twice already."

"Why not ask them to guess what it's cost to make and furnish?" Lesley Pitt suggested.

"Talk sense! How could we possibly? We're being given all sorts of things towards it. Matey's providing the stuff for curtains and bedding, and Audrey's making the carpets out of scraps of wool that anyone will give her. You couldn't *possibly* know how much they would be likely to cost," Nella said sensibly. "That won't do, anyhow."

The rest began to try to think of something, and many and weird were the suggestions produced, from Nancy Chester's awful idea that competitors should guess the complete area of the house with all its compartments and furnishings, to pretty, fluffy-headed Rosalie Browne's inspiration that this year people should be asked to *suggest* a name, and then the school at large should vote on it, the name gaining most votes to win the house itself.

"Oh, come off it!" was Julie Lucy's reaction to this. "How do you know that a dozen people wouldn't all pitch on the same name? What would you do then, may I ask?"

It was into the ensuing argument that Polly Winterton marched, in a very black mood indeed. She had just come from a fierce battle with Miss Burn, who had been instructed to give her remedial exercises as she was growing very quickly, and being a long-backed mortal, there was a slight inclination to curvature of the spine. Polly loathed the exercises, and therefore Miss Burn.

In addition, everything had gone wrong with her lessons in the morning. Her Latin exercise had been returned a mass of red ink; she had answered exactly twice during the literature lesson; in algebra, she had replied to Miss Slater's strictures so rudely that she had been sent out to cool her heels in the corridor for the remainder of the lesson, and had been caught there by Miss Annersley, who had swiftly reduced her to the size, to quote herself, of a black-beetle, and then marched her in to apologize very completely

112

to the irate mistress. Polly hated having to apologize at any time, and to have to do it with the entire form looking on induced a state of fury in her. Dinner, or Mittagessen as the school was trying to learn to call it in preparation for the time when they would remove to the Alps once more, had been cottage pie and suet duff with jam, both of which things Polly disliked. The alternative to the duff was rice pudding and stewed apple, and she hated rice. Therefore, when she walked in, it was with a brow so black that a few of the more thoughtful people hastily decided in their own minds to leave her alone until she was in a sweeter temper.

Nella was not among them. All she saw was Polly Winterton coming in. She was a new girl and might have ideas that were worth while. She promptly besieged Polly with a demand that she should suggest some new form of competition for the doll's house Tom Gray was making and she herself furnishing with help from most of the others.

"Haven't an idea," Polly said shortly, in reply to her.

"Oh, but do try to think of something," Nella coaxed. "We can't make people guess the name this time, for Bill said we must find some fresher idea. Can't you think of *anything*?"

"No, I can't!" Polly snapped unamiably. "Why should I, anyhow? What's it got to do with me?"

This was too much for the rest. With one accord they hastened to explain, but as they all talked at once, it was some time before Polly managed to gather that the school held a sale every year at the end of the Easter term, the proceeds going towards the great Sanatorium with which their school had always been connected— sometimes, unhappily, all too closely.

"The first year Tom came, she made a little house, and we made everyone pay a shilling to guess the name," Vanna said.

"The name," Nancy Chester put in with a giggle, "was 'Tomadit'—Tom Made It'—all rolled into one. We made up a list, you see, for people to choose from, and that was Mrs Maynard's idea. Tom *had* made it."

113

"Then the next year," someone else chimed in, "Tom got the wrong colour to enamel it, and it came out pillar-box red. Jacynth Hardy was Head Girl then, and when she saw the thing she stared with all her eyes and stuttered, 'b-but it's—it's s-s-*scarlet*!' So we called it 'Sacarlet' because in a way that was what it had sounded like. Wasn't Tom mad, though!" Lesley Pitt doubled up with delighted laughter as she remembered Tom's wrath, and the rest shouted with her.

"It wasn't really so bad in the end," Vanna said, when she was grave again. "Tom painted the roof black when she saw what had happened, and it really was awfully effective."

"Bit weird for a house, though," Annis Lovell interjected.

"You've said it! But it was after that that Bill said we'd got to get some new idea for the comp and we're absolutely stuck. No one can think of a single sensible thing. See if *you* can—do!" It was Elfie who wound up.

By this time Polly was forgetting that she had a deep and bitter grudge against all her world, and becoming definitely intrigued. "I see," she said; and began to think. "What's the house to be like this year?"

"Wait till we start Hobbies after prep and we'll get Tom to show you. It really is marvellous this year, and far bigger than ever before. She's simply wizard at carpentry, you know. By the way," Primrose Day went on, wouldn't *you* like a hand in it? You paint rather decently, don't you? Why don't you paint some of the pictures for it?"

Polly sat down on the back of the big chesterfield and contemplated the toes of her slippers. "Would Tom like it?" she asked dubiously. "I don't know her—not much, anyhow."

"Tom would be tickled pink," Vanna said decidedly.

"Oh, Polly, do!" Nella was at her most coaxing. "Your art work is definitely wizard; don't you think so, Clem?"

Clem Barrass, daughter of a well-known artist, though

she was only very average herself, nodded. "Polly's got a real gift; there's no doubt about it."

"What *sort* of pictures would it want?" Polly demanded, flushing plum colour at this stately compliment.

"Oh, views, and groups of flowers, and things like that," Nella said vaguely. "They'd have to be tiny, of course, so I don't see that you could manage story pictures, though it would be super if you could. What about it?"

"I could have a shot." By this time Polly was forgetting her many grievances against life, and was keenly interested. She had hitherto gone to Hobbies, mainly because she had to do so; but beyond messing about with her stamp album, she had done little or nothing. She had been so unapproachable that the others had been warned off, and it was only the necessity for finding some new form of competition, and Nella's eagerness, which had sent them to her.

"I wish you would!" Nella pressed her point home. "It would make the house all that much better if we had *real* little pictures, instead of cut-outs from Christmas cards or cigarette cards, as we did for the other two."

Polly could see that for herself. "Well, if you think you and Tom would really like it——"

"What's that I've got to like?" Tom Gay herself demanded, as she strode into the room.

Nella explained, and she nodded. "Sound scheme if you can do it. Have a stab at it, Polly. I'll show you the house—as far as it's gone—before Hobbies to-night, and then you'll have some idea of the size. Don't forget your pictures ought to have frames, if it's only cardboard and cellophane."

They had to go for tea then, and after tea came prep and supper; but once those were out of the way, Hobbies followed for two hours. Polly, armed with her pencil-box, paint-box, and a big sheet of Whatman water-colour paper she had bought from Stationery, joined gaily in the queue to the form-room where they generally worked.

Hobbies had been begun very early in the history of the school. At first the idea had been to encourage the

115

girls to interest themselves in various collections. Handcrafts had followed almost as a matter of course, and then it had been suggested that they should, as a school, try to support one of the free beds at the great Sanatorium on the far side of the Tiern See, where both school and Sanatorium had been founded. So had the annual sale been inaugurated, and the girls had turned their various hobbies to good account.

When the school had left Tirol, the Sanatorium had been obliged to leave too—or that part of it that was not Austrian—and as soon as it was firmly established among the Welsh mountains, the doctors and nursing staff had demanded that the school should renew its sale of work, and the school had been only too pleased.

They had done quite well at the last sale; but for the coming one Tom, who was nothing if not ambitious, had decided to make a regular mansion. Nella Ozanne, whose undoubted gift for carving and fretwork was to be properly trained later, had undertaken to supply the furniture; and some of the others whose tastes lay in other directions would be responsible for carpets, bedding, curtains, and so on. As a final touch, they had decided that the house should have occupants this year. Some of them had been experimenting with papier-mache work, and one or two had volunteered to try to make little heads if others would supply the bodies. Whether this last vaulting effort would come off or not remained to be seen. In fact, all the Fifths were having a hand in the matter, and if they succeeded in accomplishing all they suggested; Miss Annersley had told them that they must charge at least two shillings entrance for their competition.

Polly went eagerly to Upper Fifth with Tom while the others were settling down to their various activities, and gazed in startled silence at the house. Tom had taken her tea-chests to pieces, planed them smooth, and cut the dovetails to fit in to a frame, so that side and front and back could all be swung open. Inside, she explained, she was dividing it up into four rooms on the bottom floor, two on each side of the hall, from which she wanted to make a staircase rise to the next floor which would also have four rooms, and a little bathroom over the door. In the roof, which was to be of raffia in imitation of thatch, and have two dormer windows at the front, and windows at the side under the eaves, she proposed to make two more —hence the need for making the sides open as well as the back and front. Such a plan would have been far beyond most girls of her age, but Tom had served a long apprenticeship to carpenter's tools, and was quite capable of it.

"You see," she said to the breathless Polly, "those sitting-rooms will be only a foot square and a foot high, so you can't make your pictures too big. I should think four for the dining-room, and six for the drawing-room; and the little breakfast-room might have four too. Suppose you start off with those, and we'll consider the bedrooms when they're done?"

"I'd better do two or three first," Polly said. "Then I can show them to you, and if you think they're O.K. I could go on with more."

Tom grinned. "They'll be O.K., I'll bet. Well, in that case we know where we are, and you'd better get cracking. Hobbies lasts only two hours. Don't forget to allow for frames, will you?"

"Got it all fixed?" Primrose demanded, as she entered the room.

Polly nodded. "Yes; I'm to make a start on the dining-room pictures."

Polly, having got her water, sat down, set out paper, pencils, and rubber, and then began to consider the subject of her first picture. It should be a landscape, she thought. That wouldn't be easy, but she remembered one that she had often drawn for Lala and Freddy. It consisted of mountain slopes round a lake, with a tiny sailing-boat at one side. It was easily drawn, and she thought she could manage to colour it if she had some sort of copy to go on. She glanced round. Sitting next to her was Julie Lucy, who was busy with a super-fine scrapbook of the kind that always sold well. The pages were made of cotton material,

117

starched stiffly, and stretched tightly on a board. As each sheet was finished, it was varnished over with clear varnish, so that it could be sponged when necessary. When enough sheets had been done, they were strongly sewn into covers that some of the others made of pasteboard, covered with remnants of flowery cretonne.

Julie was a neat-fingered creature. She was using Christmas cards for the centres of her pages, and round them she arranged pictures she had cut out of magazines or other cards, and surrounded the whole with wreaths made of cut-outs from wallpapers with floral designs. At the moment, she was frowning over a charming view of a lake at sunset, and a horse's head set in a wreath of holly. She looked up, and caught Polly's glance.

"Which would *you* choose?" she asked, exhibiting her cards. "The lake is lovely; but I wonder if small kids would like the horse."

"I'd choose the lake myself," Polly said thoughtfully. "I say, Julie, if you fix on the horse's head, may I borrow the other for the colours? I won't hurt it, and I'll let you have it back as soon as I can."

Julie handed it over. "Here you are. And you needn't *bust* yourself to finish with it. I've piles more—all this hat-box full." You can look through and see if there are any more you'd like too."

"Ta awfully!" Polly took the card, glared at it for a minute or two, and then set to work with ruler and compasses to measure her frame.

For the next half-hour she worked with complete absorption. By that time she had her picture drawn, for it was a very simple affair. She made it two inches long and an inch and a half wide, allowing half an inch each way for the frame, which she meant to cut out of cardboard, and if she could get some gilding, to gild it. She sat back and looked at her outlines thoughtfully. The sketches she had tossed off at home had been quickly and carelessly done. She had taken pains with this, though, and if only she didn't make a mess of the painting, she thought it might satisfy Tom and Nella. Very carefully, she gave

118

it a first wash of watery yellow ochre, and then laid her brush down. She could do no more at it until the wash dried.

Julie saw her idle, and at once claimed her help. "Hi, Polly Winterton! You're doing nothing. Just give me a hand, will you? I've got all these dogs. Would you fill two pages with them, or spread them about through the book, so to speak?"

Polly considered, turning over the pictures. "I think I'd scatter them about. You've heaps here. I'd put two or three on a page. How big are you making the book?"

"Ten double sheets to make twenty pages. They're meant for quite small kids, so if they're much thicker they're too big for them to handle. O.K., I'll spread them about. Want to see what I've finished?" She handed over six sheets, and Polly looked at them delightedly.

"I say! They *are* smashing——"

"'Ware fines!" Julie warned her. "That's one word we're definitely not allowed to use, and you never know when some pree won't be on the prowl. They're making an awful fuss this term about slang," she added in injured tones.

As if to give point to her remark, the door opened, and Peggy Bettany and Daphne Russell appeared.

"Hello!" Peggy said cheerfully. "Everyone all right? Any help needed?"

"No, ta," Vanna replied thoughtlessly. "All the same, now you're here, you might as well give our work a dekko."

Peggy gave her a quick look. Mrs. Ozanne and Mrs. Bettany were close friends, and in the holidays the two families often visited each other, and were like one. At the same time, Vanna's greeting in present circumstances verged on impertinence to a prefect. Vanna caught the look, knew what she was thinking, and reddened to the roots of her black curls.

"Sorry, Peggy," she said. "I wasn't thinking. I didn't mean that for cheek."

"I hope not," Peggy said drily, and Vanna went redder than ever. Having duly squashed her, Peggy turned to Primrose. "What lovely work, Primrose! That tea-cloth is going to be a picture when it's done."

Primrose laughed as she spread it out to show the sprays of poppies, cornflowers, and marguerites, worked in coloured silks in the corners of the pale yellow linen. They were beautifully worked, and the colours well-chosen.

Peggy gave the work back, and passed on to Audrey Simpson, who was at work on one of the carpets for the house. She was using tapestry canvas, and, with a crochet hook and all the oddments of knitting wool she could beg, was making a "hooked" carpet. It had a cream ground with a border in three shades of blue. Peggy's eyes widened when she saw it, and she exclaimed:

"Audrey! What a simply marvellous idea! It's exactly like the kind of rugs my mother made for her bedroom last year. How *did* you think of it?"

"Same thing," Audrey said. "Mother was making a hearthrug for the drawing-room, and I wondered if I could possibly manage something like it for our house."

"But how do you measure your wool?"

Audrey produced a broken ruler. "I wind it round this. It's the smallest length I can deal with. It's finnicky work, of course, but I think it's worth it."

"Show Peggy the one you did for the nursery," Nella said. "It's super, Peggy; honestly, it is!"

Audrey opened a dress box, and took out the little carpet, which was of pale grey with pink and blue spots dotted all over it.

"But how on earth did you get it like this?" Peggy asked as she felt it. "It's like real pile, only very fine."

"When I'd finished the woolwork, and bound the back, I went over the surface, clipping it down with very sharp scissors until I got it to the right height," Audrey explained.

"It's a really admirable idea," Peggy said. "Daph!" to that individual who was at the far side of the room, admiring the fairy sheets and pillow-cases two other people had been making for the house. "Come and look at this!"

Daphne came and admired, and Audrey, a rather shy, quiet girl, was blushing by the time the two prefects had finished and moved on to admire Julie's scrapbook. Then they came to a halt behind Polly's chair. where that young person was carefully washing in a sunset sky.

Daphne stooped to look. "What are you doing, Polly? Is it a picture for the house? My dear, it's absolutely wizard! Peg, just look at this!" For Peggy had turned to admire the yacht pin-cushions Gisel Mensch had made.

She turned back, and looked down at the little picture. Polly was still painting, for she was afraid of a hard line if she stopped. Just as Peggy bent down to it, she put the last brushstroke on it, and sat back, and the Head Girl had a clear view. As Clem had said, Polly had a real gift, and the little picture bade fair to be as good in its way as Audrey's carpet or Nella's beautiful furniture.

"If you folk go on like this," Peggy said with approval, "this year's house is going to be a complete marvel. You really are making something worth while of it." She stopped short and gazed into space, frowning darkly.

"What now?" Daphne demanded, after a quick glance at her friend.

"Why, this. Suppose when the house is quite finished —fitted up in every possible way—and you people still have time over, why don't you go on making these things to sell separately?"

"My dear! What a wizard idea!" Daphne exclaimed. "You know, I really do feel you've got something there."

"You mean," Vanna cried—she was rarely suppressed for long—"have a pile of carpets like they do in shops for people to choose from for the houses they have at home."

"Oh, and boxes with pairs of curtains!" someone else added.

"Yes; and if Polly can go on with the pictures, we could rig up lines to hang them from," Peggy replied, enlarging on her idea.

"And you folk who are making sheets and pillow-cases

121

could fill other boxes, and sell them at so much a pair," Daphne chimed in.

"I could embroider some tiny counterpanes." This was Primrose.

"We-ell," Nella confessed, "I *had* meant to make lots of odd chairs and tables and beds when I'd finished the house. People don't always want to buy a whole set, and B—I mean Miss Wilson—makes me put such prices on them, and no one's a millionaire these days; but I thought they mightn't mind spending sixpence on an odd chair; or a shilling on a table or a bed."

"It's an *excellent* idea." Daphne brought the hurricane of ideas to a standstill. "Girls! I'm sure you could do awfully well out of a stall of that kind! You'll probably find you can think of quite a number of things besides all those we've mentioned——"

"I can think of one now!" Pat Collins remarked. "What about making little matresses and pillows to sell as sets? We could make them all sizes, and sell them for a few pence up to half a crown for really big bed sizes."

"Well, there you are," said Peggy. "That's just the sort of thing I mean."

The prefects left after that, to see what other people were doing; but their visit had certainly galvanized the Fifth Forms. They all talked excitedly while they went on with their work, even Polly putting in her oar now and then. In the general excitement, her past attitude was forgotten, and when the bell rang and they had to clear away their things, she had almost finished her picture; *but*, and it was a big but, she had, for the first time, been well in the interests of the others. She liked the feeling amazingly. She had been one by herself, hitherto—the Lady Acetylene Lampe, in fact. Now that was forgotten, and she was just Polly Winterton, a member of the Lower Fifth at the Chalet School.

"One thing's certain," remarked Vanna Ozanne as they finished their clearing up.

"What's that?" Dora Robson demanded.

"Well, all this will mean *work*. If we intend to have a

stall filled mainly with fiddling things like Audrey's carpets, or the sheets and things those four have been doing," she nodded towards Hilda Smith, Jane Thomas, Lorna Wills, and Jean Downes, a quartette who generally did everything together, "we'll have to dig our toes in, and hoe in at it."

"Mixed metaphor!" interjected someone. "How're you going to *hoe* if you dig your toes in at the same time? You'll overbalance!"

"Oh, dry up! You all know what I mean!" Vanna flashed.

"Get on with it, ducky, and never mind that silly ass Charmian," her twin advised. "What are you getting at?"

"Just this: we'll have to give no mistress any excuse for returning work or keeping us in or anything that will take up our time, for it strikes me, if we're going to make a real success of this stall, we'll need every moment we've got, and then some!"

Vanna stopped here, breathless with oratory and excitement.

"She's right, you know," her cousin Julie said soberly. "If we really mean to do the thing, it'll mean all that. I vote we don't just bound on the idea now, but wait till Monday and think it over. Because if we're going to do it, we're going to do it properly. *I'm* not going to have the whole school saying we've bitten off more than we could chew when the day itself comes, and so I warn you."

It was something of a wet blanket; but Julie was noted in the form for her common sense, so after some grumbling the hottest enthusiasts agreed to think it over and see if they thought they could really manage to work hard enough during school to avoid trouble with the staff, and so have their free time to themselves from then until the day of the sale.

All the same, Polly had taken note, and that night when she was curled up in bed, she vowed to herself that not only would she try to keep with the others, and not play the part of the Cat-That-Walked, but she would also do her level best with her lessons. Having made which

123

sensible decision, she turned over, snuggled down, and fell asleep, more or less reconciled to school for the moment at any rate.

Chapter Twelve

A CHANGE OF LANGUAGE

"Well, I call that a simply *smashing* idea!"

Peggy, passing along the upper corridor, caught this remark, and frowned sharply. "That's that little wretch, Blossom Willoughby," she hissed to Daphne, who was with her as usual. "You go on. I must go and tick her off for the good of her soul!"

Daphne laughed, and went on her way to their form-room, while Peggy descended the stairs with some dignity, just in time to catch her own young cousin, Sybil Russell, remark, "Smashing? I call it a complete piece of cake!"

Peggy had just come from gym, and still wore her plimsolls. Her light tread on the stairs made no sound, and the pair nearly jumped sky-high when they heard her voice. "Blossom—*and* Sybil! Why are you talking in the corridor? Don't you know the rules *yet*?"

No answer: but the pair were beetroot red. Peggy waited a moment. "Report yourselves for extra drill for breaking rules," she said at last. "And what have you been told about slang? Pay the usual fine—wait a minute, though. This isn't the first time this week by a long way. Blossom, how many fines have you had for slang since Monday?"

"Three!" muttered Blossom, looking suddenly anxious.

"And you, Sybil?"

Sybil, it seemed, had had only one—for a wonder!

More than half her pocket-money went into the fines box these days, now that the authorities had intimated that it was time the girls spoke purer English than they had been doing.

"Very well," Peggy said. "Sybil, you pay a double fine, and see that that's the last for this week. Blossom, pay a double fine, too, and remember that you mayn't ask for Bank for a fortnight." She turned to go, and some unlucky imp impelled her to add: "Perhaps that will help you two to remember that certain words are utterly forbidden here except when used with their proper meaning."

The younger pair had felt badly disgruntled at their punishment, but this gratuitous remark struck them as adding insult to injury. They could scarcely wait until they were safely in the shelter of their own form-room before they could let fly and say what they thought of the Head Girl and all her works. Peggy's ears should have burned right off before they had finished. Sybil in her rage incautiously wound up a diatribe which had all the other girls in the form-room listening with admiration for her flow of language, by calling her cousin "an inter- fering bat of a cow!" just as Miss Stephens walked in to take them for dictation, and got the full force of this pearl of oratory. Miss Stephens took Sybil by the shoulder and walked her up to the mistress's table while the others scuttled or slunk to their seats, and stood her there without a word until the room was in order. Then she opened fire, and by the time she had finished, there was not much left of Miss Sybil, who was on the verge of tears long before the mistress had ended. Finally she found herself con- demned to the form of torture known as "Miss Stephens' walks," which meant that instead of having games, which she loved, she must be ready for the mistress at games time, neatly clad in hat and coat and gloves, and carrying an umbrella, and go for a prim walk when she was expected to converse politely on matters of interest. And if her ideas failed her during the walk, she had to write an essay on some subject chosen by Miss Stephens before she so much as touched any of her proper preparation

Blossom had, of course, tried to take part of the blame, but Miss Stephens had guessed some days before that between the two Fourths there existed an alliance whereby any piece of wickedness, unless it was plain that the person blamed could not possibly have had a partner in crime, should be claimed by anyone else who could have had the least hand in the matter. She was, as she told Blossom severely, quite tired of hearing the girls accuse themselves on the flimsiest grounds, and meant to have no more of it.

"You may sit down, Blossom," she wound up. "I wish to hear no more from you. Sybil's shocking language is all her own. If she chooses to use such expressions, she must pay for it—no one else."

Blossom made haste to sit down and hide her head in her book of dictation passages while the mistress finished reducing Sybil to a mere insect. It is scarcely surprising that neither of the two got a single mark for that dictation —which means staying in after four to write the passage out three times in their neatest handwriting, and having to go to "late tea," which meal was presided over by Matron, who resented such a waste of her time, and let all sinners know it. It is true that members of the Sixth frequently appeared at late tea, but theirs were legitimate excuses, and if none of the younger members of the school were present, Matron did not appear.

On this day, as it happened, Matron was very busy. There were only three detainees, and most of the Sixths were having tea in the prefects' room.

The only exception happened to be Eilunedd Vaughn, who had a late lesson on shorthand with Miss Dene, the School secretary, and who knew that tea in the prefects' room would be over by the time she arrived there, and preferred to put in an appearance at the dining-room, where she received a hearty welcome from Matron.

"Oh, Eilunedd! Would you mind seeing to these children? Miss Wilson wanted to see me at five, and it's five to five already. See that they get their meal properly and then go to change, as they were too late before. Thank you!"

Matron vanished, and Eilunedd was left with the trio—Blossom, Mary-Lou Trelawney of Upper Third, who had elected *not* to know her history—and Sybil.

For a minute or two, Eilunedd only grasped the fact that three of the younger girls had been in detention. Then she suddenly saw Sybil—Peggy Bettany's cousin!

All the term Eilunedd had nursed a smouldering grudge against the innocent Peggy. It had grown until, so far as the Head Girl was concerned, she really could not see straight. It would be difficult for her to deal with her as she had done with Gwensi Howell some terms before. Peggy was far too much a general favourite for that. At the same time she was determined that the term should not end without the Head Girl realising that she was a usurper. She wondered, as she poured out fresh tea for Blossom and Mary-Lou, if she could get at her through Sybil.

"More tea, Sybil?" she said presently, holding out her hand for Sybil's cup.

Sybil passed it with a muttered, "Yes, please."

Eilunedd filled the cup, handed it back, and helped herself to a bun. With a sudden impulse, she held out the plate towards the three. "Here, you may as well have one each," she said casually. "I'm the only Sixth Former likely to be here, and it's a pity to send a full plate back to the kitchen."

Blossom, who was as heedless as a girl of thirteen could well be, promptly took one, saying, "Thank you, Eilunedd."

Sybil hesitated. Buns were never meant for people who were kept in.

"Go on!" her chum said, giving her a nudge.

Sybil flushed. Then she took the bun with a murmured, "Thank you." But when the plate was passed to Mary-Lou, that downright young person shook her head. "Thanks awfully, Eilunedd, but I've been in deten, so I can't, worse luck!"

Eilunedd laughed. "Oh, go on, Mary-Lou. It's quite all right for once."

But Mary-Lou still refused. "No; that wasn't what Miss Bell meant when she told me to stay in and go to late tea. Anyhow, I asked for it," she added philosophically.

Sybil ate her bun; but she hardly enjoyed it. She knew well enough that neither had Miss Stephens expected it when she and Blossom were kept in. She stole a glance at Blossom, but that young woman was munching away cheerfully, and reflecting that they were 'one up' on Miss Stephens. Eilunedd saw the glance, but she said nothing. A plan was beginning to grow in her mind, and she needed time to think it out. No point in starting an argument about the buns. She put the plate down on the table with that light laugh of hers, and told Mary-Lou to take some more bread-and-butter if she wouldn't have a bun.

Eilunedd finished her own tea, and sat watching until her juniors had finished theirs. She said Grace for them and saw them out of the dining-room after bidding them hurry up and change or they would be late for prep.

"And I suppose none of you want that," she added.

They fled to their dormitories, and managed to be down in time for preparation, looking very neat and trim in their winter evening frocks of dark brown velvet with muslin collars and cuffs.

Mary-Lou went off to Upper Third and Blossom and Sybil made their way to the long narrow room which belonged to Upper Fourth.

"Hard luck on you two," remarked Gwen Parry as they entered. "Did Matey have much to say?"

"Matey wasn't there—or not after the very beginning," Blossom informed her. "Eilunedd landed in and Matey handed us over to her. I say, you know," she went on heedlessly, "Eilunedd's not half bad. She gave us a bun each. Said she was the only Sixther there and it was a pity to send back a full plate to the kitchen. So we were one up on Steffy this time!"

"But, I say," began Gwen in startled tones, "you aren't supposed to——"

Blossom stopped her. "Oh, not if Steffy knows, of course," she said with a giggle. "In fact, that little ass

Mary-Lou said so, more or less. But after all, Eilunedd's Special Sixth, and she *was* a pree last year. We're supposed to treat the Specials like prees, aren't we? Well, then!"

"Well, if Eilunedd did it, I suppose it's all right," Gwen said doubtfully.

"All right? Of course it's all right. Help! There's the first bell and I haven't a thing ready." Blossom stopped gossiping, and made for the lockers at the side of the room to disinter the books she needed for the evening, and Sybil followed her.

Unlike Blossom, she was not particularly heedless, and after Gwen's remarks, she could not help feeling that however much of a Special Sixth Eilunedd was, she had had no right to take that bun. Anyhow, she knew her mother would have said so; and so would Auntie Jo.

Later on, when they were all free to amuse themselves as they liked till bedtime, Upper and Lower Fourth, who shared a common-room perforce, drew together to discuss the subject of the latest ban on slang.

Blossom suddenly said: "I've got an idea."

They crowded round her at once. "Oh, what is it?"

"Go on, Blossom! Tell us, if it's anything that'll save us from fines. I've scarcely a penny left," Meg Whyte said eagerly.

"Well, it's just this. You know the day of the storm?"

"Yes—go on!" they urged.

"Well, we were over at art when the Sixth were having some lessons there too. Joan Sandys sat on Nina Williams for using slang, and she said——"

"Who did—Nina or Joan?" someone demanded.

"Nina did. She said it was hard lines to have to talk like a Jane Austen heroine, but she'd do her best. And then Peggy was down on her like a knife. Said they wouldn't have any of her 'vastly' and—and—'monstrous,' and all that."

"Well, what's that got to do with us?" Pat asked as Blossom paused.

"Why, don't you see, you cake, it can't be slang, or Jane Austen wouldn't have written it. Miss Annersley said in a lesson to us that she wrote clear, precise English. "I vote we all begin to talk like that."

"But how could we?" Sybil demanded. "I've only read bits of *Pride and Prejudice* and *Northanger Abbey*. I liked them all right, but when I got the book I was awfully browned off with it."

"Well, we'll just have to read them now," Blossom said. "Never mind being browned off. We'll just have to stick it till we see how they did talk in those days."

"What are you kids talking about?"

They turned and saw Eilunedd standing in the doorway. One or two of them looked at each other guiltily. How much had she overheard?

Eilunedd paid no heed to them just then. She glanced round the room till her eyes lighted on Gwen Parry, for whom she was looking.

"Gwen Parry," she said, "Matron wants to see you in her room. Hurry on!"

Gwen flushed. Matron had caught her sneezing that evening, and had bidden her come for a dose of the school's own particular brand of cold cure. Gwen had conveniently forgotten all about it till then, and she guessed Matey would have something to say. She scurried out of the room, and Eilunedd turned to Blossom.

"What were you talking about when I came in?" she asked curiously.

"Just—how did people talk in Jane Austen's time; and Sybil said her books were—were fearfully dull," Blossom replied.

"Well, so, for kids like you, I imagine they are," Eilunedd agreed. "If you want to read any books about that time, why don't you try Georgette Heyer's. There are two or three in the library, and they are quite interesting, and would tell you all you want to know about the language of that time. But why *do* you want to know, anyway?"

Blossom opened her mouth to answer; but Hilary was too quick for her. Better not leave it to her, for you never knew what she might say! Therefore Hilary replied most sedately: "We were talking about the different kinds of slang. You know *we* say things are 'wizard', or 'super.' But Mummy says she used to say, 'Topping' or 'top-hole,' or 'absolutely It'. And Granny once told me she got into an awful row for saying something was 'ripping.' We thought we'd like to know how people talked ages before that."

Eilunedd's eyebrows shot up at this. However, she merely remarked: "Well, Georgette Heyer's books would give you some idea. I quite agree that Jane Austen is probably beyond you at present. Meanwhile I'd advise you to cut out quite so much of 'super' in your chat. It verges on forbidden slang, as you ought to know." Then she strolled from the room, having given them something to think about.

The result of all this was that when Upper Fourth went to change their books, they took out all of Georgette Heyer's they could find. Among them they contrived to make some sort of a vocabulary that would have passed muster among folk in the very early years of the nineteenth century, though it took them the best part of a week to manage it. When they were alone, they practised it on each other, frequently dissolving into fits of laughter over it. When the next Saturday came, however, they decided that they could manage enough for their purpose.

Accordingly, Peggy and Nina, coming downstairs for breakfast, were electrified to hear Sybil, who had taken to this new amusement with avidity, address Lala as 'You foolish rattle!' and desire her to cease from 'funning.'

"What on *earth*——" Nina paused.

"No idea," Peggy said tersely. "'Tisn't slang, though, so we can't do much about it—*yet*!"

At nine o'clock the school retired to its form-rooms to do mending, such preparation as they had not finished the day before, and write their home letters. They were not allowed to talk for the first hour out of mercy for those who were still doing home-work. After that they might if they did it quietly. The prefects sat with the Middles, and on this occasion, Upper Fourth was supervised by Frances Coleman, known among her own crowd as

'Blunderbuss,' for if there was a thing it was wiser not to say or do, she was almost certain to produce it. All the same, she was a favourite with most folk, being good-natured in the extreme, and willing to give a hand to anyone.

Upper Fourth worked hard for the first hour. They were not *very* sure just how the prefects would regard their latest attempt at livening things up, and they were not minded to have to give any part of the afternoon to work.

By ten o'clock, even Hilda Jukes, who was lag of the form though she did her best, had managed to finish all her work. A general air of relaxation took the place of the fierce absorption which had reigned previously.

Blossom Willoughby put away her writing materials, and took out a blouse that needed two buttons. She threaded her needle, fished for her buttons, and then, with one eye cocked to see how Frances would take it, opened the ball.

"Oh, Sybil," she said gently but clearly, "I wish you will lend me a thimble. I have forgot mine."

"I would if I could," Sybil replied sweetly, "but I have but the one, and if I lend you that, I am utterly undone."

Frances, mending a ripped glove, frowned to herself. What were those imps up to? It wasn't slang, exactly, but—— She glanced up and caught Sybil's eye, and that young woman went exceedingly red. However, the prefect's attention was drawn from her by Hilary Wilson, who was a scamp of the first water. She and her boon companion Meg Whyte had been whispering together. Now Hilary sat back with a giggle.

"I don't believe you!" she said. "You're bamming me—or trying to."

Frances was jerked to the upright at this remark. "Hilary Wilson!" she said severely, "you *know* slang is forbidden. Pay your fine to the box, and don't say that again."

Hilary straightened her quivering lips, but imps danced in her eyes as she replied very properly: "If you please, Frances, I did not know it was slang. I read it in a story about—about——"

"The Regency, you boob!" hissed Meg.

"Oh yes; the Regency, Frances."

Frances was floored. She was no reader herself, and found the books she must read for literature quite enough. It seemed hardly possible that novels dealing with that particular period would be slangy; at the same time she felt fairly certain that the expression was hardly a polite one.

"It was a very pretty tale," Hilary continued: and Frances felt more bewildered than ever. Never, in the whole course of her school career, had she heard a girl describe a story as 'pretty.' What *were* the wretched kids up to?

"Very well," she said at last. "I'll remit the fine this time, but don't use it again. You may sit down and go on with your work."

Hilary sat down meekly, but under her lowered lashes her blue eyes gleamed with wickedness.

The next shock came from Gwen Parry, who was form prefect, and generally did her best to keep her crowd up to the mark. On this occasion, however, Gwen was smarting under the loss of sixpence of her precious weekly shilling for using various slang terms, and she had joined in the scheme with glee. Madge Watson was sitting sucking the end of her pen, and cudgelling her brains for something more to fill up her sheet, since she had not the pen of a ready writer.

Gwen leaned across and skimmed over what she had written. Then she sniffed scornfully. "What a gudgeon you are, Madge! You have said nothing of our Hobbies Club; nor mentioned our last carol practice!"

"Why, I vow I had forgot them all," Madge replied. "I thank you, Gwen, for your reminder. Pray tell me if there should be anything else, for my parents are shockingly angered at me if I do not send them two pages."

It was quite clear to Frances that this was a put-up job, and she laid down her glove, rapped on the table with her thimble, and when everyone was looking at her, said sharply: "Now listen to me! You girls are to talk the

King's English and not—not rubbish like this," she concluded lamely.

The girls looked at each other. Blossom finally spoke.

"But, if you please, Frances," she said—and oh! how prim she looked!—"we have been told to use words in their proper meaning, and indeed we are but trying to do so. Do, pray, explain where we are gone wrong. Indeed, we all wish you will do so."

Silence! Frances' wits were not quick enough to deal with demons like Blossom Willoughby and her crew. Apart from Hilary's extraordinary expression, no one had said a single thing that could be remotely regarded as slang, and she could scarcely see how she could pull them up for suddenly beginning to talk in the style that was fashionable a hundred and twenty or thirty years earlier. Moreover, there was nothing in Blossom's manner to which she could legally object, though she felt that the young monkey was making fun of her in some subtle way. She must do something quickly, though, so she merely said: "You heard what I said. Now go on with your letters, and don't let me have any more nonsense!" Blossom sat down, the very picture of a good little girl; and for the last ten minutes or so, there was peace. But once the bell for Elevenses had rung, and the Middles had all streamed off to the kitchen, Frances scrambled her possessions together anyhow, and fled upstairs to inform the others of the very latest, and ask what they could do about it.

Peggy listened with a serious face, but when Frances solemnly informed them of Hilary's remark, she could contain herself no longer and she broke into peals of laughter.

"The *imps*!" she said, when she was grave again. "The outrageous *imps*! However, we'll be even with them. This is to pay us back for all the fines they've had lately for slang. I wonder who was the genius who thought of it? All right, Frances: don't you worry. And, by the way, you can tell young Hilary that fine is *not* remitted. 'Bamming' was Regency slang for—for 'pulling one's

134

leg.' I rather think it was short for 'bamboozle,' but I'm not sure. Thank goodness this is a week-end. I'll just get my cocoa and biscuits, and then I'll see if I can see one of the Heads. In the meantime, just listen, all of you, and see if you can find out which forms are in it."

"Have an idea?" Daphne asked eagerly.

Peggy nodded. "They're going to be sorry they ever tried this game on! But we've got to see what the Head says first. Look here; someone snaffle my cocoa, and I'll go straight to the study now." And with this she was off.

She rejoined them ten minutes later, and her dancing eyes told them that she had obtained permission for her scheme. In the meantime, they had all used their ears well, and had learned that it was the two Fourths who were responsible for the sudden change of language.

"I *thought* so!" quoth Peggy. "It generally *is* the Fourths who try to play up. Well, we'll pay them back in their own coin and see how they like it. Most fortunately, it's been too wet for any games and everyone is going for a walk. No time now—there's the bell, and it's Guides. I'll tell you the details after."

With this they had to be content; but judging by the yells of laughter that drifted from the prefects' room when they were free, Peggy's plan was funny, and they expected a good deal of amusement from it. They parted to change from Guide uniforms into skirts and blouses for the afternoon, and the two Fourth Forms, religiously keeping up their plot, had no idea what horrid things were in store for them as soon as Mittagessen was over.

Chapter Thirteen

PEGGY SCORES!

Mittagessen was almost ended when the bell from the Heads' table sounded, and the girls stopped chattering and turned to look at Miss Annersley, wondering what she wanted to say to them.

"The playing-fields are so wet," she said, "that there can be no games this afternoon, I'm afraid. Even the en-tout-cas court has pools lying all over it. You girls will have an hour and a half's walk instead. Seniors, you may take the ferry and cross to Carnbach if you like. Special Sixth will go with you. Be sure you don't miss the four o'clock ferry back, though. Some of the mistresses are going on their own account, so they will see you safely over, and meet you at the landing at five to four. The two Thirds may go round to the Cove by the village. Miss Stephens and Miss Burn are taking the three Second forms in the other direction. Kindergarten, your own mistresses are taking you to the spinney and back, so be sure you all put on wellingtons and raincoats, and try to keep out of puddles." She gave the excited little girls a smile. Then she became grave again, and looked round. "The two Fourths will take their walk with some of the prefects who have a plan for them, and will see them about it after Mittagessen. Now, has everyone finished? Stand, please, for Grace."

The girls all stood up and she said Grace. Then she headed the long line of mistresses from the room, and Peggy, as soon as Miss Bell, the newest comer to the school, had passed through the top door, took charge.

"Will everyone except the two Fourths please go and

136

get ready at once?" she said. "Fourth Form girls, remain in your places."

Such members of those two forms as were near enough, exchanged glances. But Peggy was speaking again, so they listened.

"I understand," she said, "that you have been using —er—Regency language. As this period seems to interest you, we thought it a pity you shouldn't—shouldn't carry the thing out properly;"—Peggy only just stopped herself from saying, 'Going the whole hog'; but she felt that even the most innocent slang was best avoided just then— "so we have decided that for the whole week-end you are to behave as if you were schoolgirls at that period. I'm sorry we can't arrange for you to wear the same kind of clothes; but we *can* see that you take the kind of walks they used to have, and the same kind of occupations. For instance," Peggy went on blandly, "to-morrow in the afternoon, you are to occupy yourselves by learning the catechism—part of it."

She stopped there, mainly to get hold of herself, for the Middles were staring at her with such horror in their faces that it was almost more than she could do to keep a straight face. When she was sure that her voice was steady again, she went on.

"In those days, children were expected to *listen* to the sermon in church, and when they returned home, many of them were required to write down as much as they could remember of it. *You* will do that after church to-morrow. This evening, you are to bring your needlework to the prefects' room, and while you sew, one of us will read aloud to you. Also, for supper you will have what girls of that day would have had—bread-and-milk."

At this final pronouncement, a gasp of sheer disgust went round the room. All the same, no one, not even Blossom, dared say anything. And fortunately for the prefects, not one of the Middles even suspected how near the big girls were to collapsing into peals of laughter. Peggy waited a minute to see if anyone had anything to say. Finding that they had not—or not to her, at any rate—she told them to go and get ready. They were to wear coats, caps, gloves, and wellingtons.

"Even on the highroad there will be pools after all the rain there has been, and you must be careful to avoid wet feet," Peggy said sweetly.

"And just see that your hats are on straight and you are *tidy*," Frances added startlingly; but she was still annoyed about Hilary. "Girls in those days were always expected to be very spick and span."

The Fourths knew better than to answer back, but they all felt that she had added insult to injury, and it made them no better disposed towards their elders and betters. Very disgruntled, they left the room and made for the Splasheries, where they changed their slippers, pulled on their hats and coats, and finally wriggled their hands into their gloves.

At last they were ready, and all waiting for the prefects on the paved path at the side of the house. Five of the elder girls came, the others having gone to Carnbach with the rest of the Seniors. Peggy, Daphne, Dickie, Joan, and Frances walked primly round the corner and surveyed their victims.

"Sybil, my love," her cousin said gently, "Your hair is not as neat as becomes a young lady. Nor is Lala's— nor Hilary's," she added, with a quick glance round. "To-morrow, I shall expect to see a vast improvement in your appearance. To-day, as we are late already, I will pardon it. But where, pray, are your umbrellas? You had best carry them lest it should rain and you would then be wet. Pray bring them and make haste."

No one dared to object aloud; but they all felt that this was the finishing touch. *Umbrellas*, if you please! And there wasn't a cloud in the sky—or no rain-clouds, anyhow! Sybil gave Peggy a look of fury, and met one in return that was all sweetness, but with something behind the sweetness that reminded her that Peggy was Head Girl as well as her cousin. Seething with rage, she went meekly with the others to bring her loathed umbrella, and when they were all back, accepted as her partner for the walk Iris Harris, a girl from Lower Fourth whom she had once characterized to her own chums as 'an empty-headed ass of a giggler'! Her own particular chum, Blossom, had been presented with Freda Lund, also from Lower Fourth, and was two or three couples away from her. In fact, as Sybil found when she thought it over, the prefects had mixed up their lambs very thoroughly, and no girl was anywhere near her chosen friends. Peggy led the way, and Daphne brought up the rear, accompanied by Lala Winterton and Gwen Parry. The other prefects came between, each with her escort of a girl from each form.

At first the long crocodile went in silence; but once they had left the Big House grounds, Peggy turned her head.

"You may converse," she said solemnly, "so long as you do it in ladylike tones, and ladylike language. Pray be careful to avoid pools."

They plodded along the highway, most of them thinking things not lawful to be uttered. The prefects set them an example by talking quietly to their escorts in the most ultra-refined language, and slowly the rebels yielded, and began to talk themselves. It wasn't easy, though, with the big girls listening for any approach to modern slang; and Sybil and Blossom, at any rate, more than once had to break off what they were saying, for they really could not express themselves without using terms and phrases that they knew might bring some further weird and awful punishment on their heads.

"Pray, Sybil, do but look where you are going," Dickie observed at this point, smothering a giggle as she spoke. She was a blunt person by nature, and she found it not only funny, but distinctly an effort to remember that she *must* talk as much like a Jane Austen heroine as she could.

Sybil knew nothing of this as she drew to one side of an enormous puddle. The so-called highroad was badly in need of repairs, and the continuous rain of the past week had left pools everywhere.

Blossom was beginning to recover from her initial dismay at their ordeal. She turned to Freda, who was a sedate young person of thirteen, and said with a smothered titter: "Pray, Freda, are you not bored with this road? I wish we might go by the cliffs."

Freda went pink. "So do I!" she said fervently.

Joan overheard them, and grinned to herself, but she said nothing, except to rebuke Meg Whyte sharply for swinging her umbrella in a nonchalant manner.

"Pray carry your umbrella properly, Meg," she said. "Your conduct with it hardly beseems a young gentlewoman."

All in all, that was one of the most unpleasant walks the two forms ever took, and by the time it was over, and they were safely back in Big House, they were bitterly regretting that they had ever had such a brilliant idea as had called such a horrid punishment on them. And worse was to follow. Instead of sitting as they chose for tea, they were solemnly seated round three special tables where they were feasted on thick bread-and-scrape, with a teaspoonful of jam allotted to each one, and cups of milk instead of their usual tea.

The insuppressible Blossom asked if she might not go to bring a cake from her tuck-box, but Peggy replied in shocked tones: "Indeed, no! You have good, nourishing food as it is, and jam as a treat, and I am sorry that you should be so greedy, Blossom." Whereat Blossom blushed to the roots of her hair, and wished she had not spoken.

Tea over, they were sent upstairs to change for the evening, and directed to bring their needlework with them, and while the rest were enjoying themselves dancing and playing games after supper, the fifty-odd who composed the two forms were sitting sulkily going on with their sewing, while Peggy, Judy Rose, and Barbara Henschell took it in turns to read aloud to them from a hideous little book which Peggy had dug up from somewhere, entitled: *Lucy Marlowe; or the Orphan Cousins.*

When eight o'clock struck, they were told to fold up

their work neatly, and then all sent up to bed in a state of as deadly boredom and furious wrath mixed as ever they had known.

Sunday was even worse in some ways. As soon as breakfast and bed-making were over, they were sent to their form-rooms as usual to write their home-letters; but instead of being left to themselves, they were accompanied by prefects. Church meant paying full attention to the sermon, for they were warned before setting out that they would be expected to write a summary of it when they returned, and it seemed to them that never had the Rector been so prosy or so long-winded. Nor did the Catholic girls fare any better. The Friar who came over from St. Bride's, one of the smaller islands of the group, where the Dominicans had a community, seemed to have set out to be as dull as he could. The girls, listening hopefully at first for something that would make their future task easier, discovered that they had to listen carefully to the whole sermon.

"And even then I don't think I can possibly write more than three sentences about it!" wailed Elizabeth Gregory; and most of them were in the same boat.

When the afternoon came, they had half an hour during which they were set to learning sundry catechism questions by heart, and after that came another appallingly dull walk, attired in Sunday hats and coats, carrying those hated umbrellas again—this time with some excuse, since there were threatening clouds about—and 'conversing', not talking. Neither, since they were once again escorted along the highroad, might they break rank.

However, their persecutors relented a little, for they were allowed a piece of cake each for tea; and when the school assembled in Hall for Sunday night hymn-singing, they were taken to join the rest. Moreover, those whose turn it had been to choose the hymns had selected all the rousing ones they could find, and after singing 'Onward, Christian Soldiers', 'Who is She that Stands Triumphant', and several others of the same kind, the two Fourths felt definitely better. Supper came next, and after that, except for the Seniors, bed, as most of the Fourths thankfully remembered. They had had an awful day and a half, but it was over, or nearly so!

Peggy summoned them to their common-room before they went upstairs, though, and drove the lesson home.

"You folk have had a dull time of it," she said, "but perhaps it has helped to show you first how much better off we are in these days. For, you know, you've had just the sort of thing girls of the Regency expected to have every day. Secondly, I hope it's shown you just how badly you are all steeped in slang, and explained to you why you are fined for using it as you do. If it helps you to stop it, then it's been all to the good. And just remember, all you people, that every period has its own form of slang, and one kind is just as bad as another. Well, it's over now. To-morrow, you can start fair again, and do, for goodness' sake, try to reform so far as your everyday language is concerned! I can assure you it's been quite as boring for us as for you!"

She dismissed them after that, and they streamed off to bed, thankful that it was ended. Not that it was: oh dear, no! The Heads retailed the story with much gusto to Jo when she arrived for the Sixth Forms' history lessons next day, and it was not in Jo not to tease a little. She solemnly addressed the Upper Fourth, to whom she came purposely to do it, as 'Young Misses', and asked, with a wicked twinkle, if they had enjoyed 'Lucy Marlowe', as she had several more of the same kind, and would be delighted to lend them!

However, in one way, Peggy's hopes were fulfilled. For the rest of the term, the entire clan really did try to reform where slang was concerned; and if their efforts were spasmodic on the whole, at least the fines box slowly became poorer.

Chapter Fourteen

MADGE'S SURPRISE

"Given the conditions—the lack of representation in Parliament, the overbearing treatment from the Government, the stupidity of the various Governors, it is hardly wonderful that the Colonists were gradually brought to a state of seething discontent. The Stamp Act was oil on fuel, and the Tea Tax was the torch that set the whole thing ablaze—Yes? What is it, Meg?" Jo paused in her lesson to the Sixth to raise her eyebrows questioningly at Meg Whyte, who had just entered the room.

"Miss Dene asked me to tell you that Dr. Maynard is here and says he has some surprising news for you," Meg said primly.

"Oh? Thank you, Meg. I'll come." Jo nodded, and Meg departed, while the history mistress turned back to her class. "I must go, girls. I don't suppose I'll be very long. Until I return, please make notes on what I've been saying to you. If I still haven't come back by the time you've finished them, go on preparing the beginnings of the American Revolution for yourselves, making notes as you read, of course."

Jo left them after this, and they settled down to making their notes. Daphne Russell jotted down all she could remember, and then glanced at Peggy, who was looking worried.

"Meg said *surprising* news," she said in an undertone.

Peggy lifted her head from her work. She was not so quick as her friend. "I know; all the same, I do wonder what it means."

143

"If it's anything to do with your family I expect your aunt will tell you when she comes back," Daphne said soothingly.

Meanwhile, Jo herself, wildly excited by this mysterious summons, had made her way to the study, where she found her husband sitting by the fire, smoking. He gave her a grin as she came in.

"What on earth are you doing here at this time of day?" was his wife's inhospitable greeting, as she shut the door behind her.

"*Wouldn't* you like to know?" he began teasingly. Then: "Hi, leave my hair alone! *Jo!* You can't rag here. Suppose any of the kids came in and caught you? You'd look well wouldn't you?"

Jo stopped in her onslaught on his hair. "Tell me why you've come, then, and stop teasing!" Her face suddenly changed. "Jack! There's nothing wrong in Canada, is there? Margot—Madge—"

"Nothing at all," he interrupted her quickly. "Margot seems to be developing into a small giantess. As for Madge, she's one complete thrill, judging by what Jem says."

"What *do* you mean? What's been happening? You've had a letter from Jem? But this isn't mail day!" Jo lifted puzzled black eyes to his face. "How could you possibly hear from him? And anyway, you hadn't come home when I left this morning. Has he been phoning you?"

"Well, he did," her husband admitted. "But I'd got a letter before that. A pal of his was flying across two days ago, and Jem gave him a letter for me. It arrived at the San by this morning's post, with one in it for you. I thought you'd better hear the glad tidings at once, which is why I'm here."

He had sat down again, and Jo perched herself on the arm of his chair and held out her hand with one word, "Give"!

He produced a letter, addressed to her in her brother-in-law's well-known script, and gave it to her. Then he returned to his pipe while Jo ripped the envelope open, and spread out the sheets it contained. She read for a few

144

seconds only. Then she turned to her husband with a loud gasp.

"*Jack Maynard!* What do you know about *this!* Did you *ever!* Why on earth didn't they let us know sooner——"

"You read your letter and stop going off into exclamation marks like a rocket," he said with a chuckle. "No; I knew nothing about it till this morning's post. They've been uncommonly secret about it, though, haven't they ?"

Jo turned to her letter again. "Jem says *last Monday.* Even if they didn't let us know beforehand, why couldn't they tell us sooner than this?" she complained.

"If you read on I expect you'll know all about it," he replied.

"My dear Jo," Jem had written. "On the whole, I'm glad I'm nowhere near you at this moment. I know what you're like when you fly out, and you'll be ready to fly out when you've heard my news, or I miss my guess. My dear, prepare yourself for a shock. Last Monday Madge had twin sons—those brothers you've wanted for young David at long last! Madge is going on well, and the babies are splendid specimens. A weighed five pounds at birth, and B was four pounds three ounces. They gain steadily all the time, and have lungs like a blacksmith's bellows! A is fair and so, Madge says, like me. B is as dark as David was, and Madge's image.

"Madge was pretty much under the weather for a day or so at first; but she's over that now, and is making headway every day. I didn't write sooner, *nor* cable you as I expect you are cursing me for not doing, until I could report really excellent progress all round. I know you, Jo! I wouldn't have put it past you to make a dive for the first plane for Canada if I had, and we didn't want any whirlwinds around. The three girls are wild with delight, especially our two. It seems they've been very bored with having just one brother so much older than themselves. To have two at a go now is a real joy.

"Do you remember our 'Names' party for Sybil? We convened one here when I told them and they presented me with a hair-raising choice of names. Margot was set on

'Lancelot'; and Josette wanted one to be named 'Toronto' because they were born in Toronto! However, you'll be glad to hear that we have given all their ideas the go-by. The pair are to be Kevin and Kester. For good measure, Kevin will have Jack's name after Kevin, and Kester, after a good deal of argument, is to be Kester Richard, after his uncle and maternal grandfather. By the way, Madge wants me to tell you that 'Kester' is an old English form of 'Christopher'; so if you're thinking of adding to your own family don't if it's a boy, pitch on 'Christopher' for a name."

"Well, I'm not—at the moment," Jo paused in her reading to remark. "Just the same, Jack, Michael is getting a big boy now—sixteen months old!—and we ought to think about it before long. We both like big families, and I'd like at least *one* more daughter after three boys one after the other."

Jack laughed. "I thought you'd say that when you heard the news. Madge has certainly managed to catch up with you and Mollie now. If you want to keep ahead, you really ought to hurry up."

"Well, I do. I don't believe in spreading it over years as Madge has done. Poor David!" Jo laughed gently. "He'll be more like an uncle or a second father to these babies than a brother. He's nearly sixteen years older than they are. I wonder what he'll think about it?" Jo turned to her husband. "Does he know yet?"

"Jem told me in his letter that he'd written to him, and knew you would break the glad news to Sybil. Finish your letter, Jo, and don't yatter so much. Time's going on, and I've got to get back to the San to-night. We're pretty busy just now, as you know,"

" Madge says I am also to tell you that now she has levelled up with Mollie and you, she'll be satisfied. She always felt that seeing she was the eldest of the three she ought not to be behindhand in the matter of family. I have pointed out to her that after all Mollie was a mere infant when she married, and you not much better. *She* had reached the mature age of twenty-six.

"I've written to the Quadrant, so you needn't worry about them. But let the girls know they have two new cousins. David will attend to Rix and Jackie. I suppose. I've written to him. I'm leaving it to you to tell my Sybil.

"Now you know why we decided to remain in Canada for the present, though we might have done that for the children's sake even if we hadn't had any expectations.

"I rather think that when we do return your daughter to you you won't regret having spared her to us for so long. She has grown a good inch and a half, and has put on weight steadily, and has lost her look of fragility for keeps, I imagine. She sleeps well, eats well, and the only times she isn't in mischief are when she's asleep, or during her lessons. The Convent seems to be improving her both mentally and spiritually. I know you and Jack will be glad to know that we've had only one outburst of rage in all these months, and that wasn't anything to write home about. As for her lessons, I saw Soeur Marie-Cécile two days ago, and she tells me that none of the three is lacking in brains, but your Margot can beat them all hands down when she chooses. As we sent them to La Sagesse, where French is the order of the day, all three can now chatter French as glibly as English.

"Madge says I am to tell you that as soon as she feels stronger she will write you a longer letter. At present, she still spends a good deal of her time in sleeping. Tell Sybil that Mummy will write to her by the next mail, if it's only a note. The nuns are keeping her very quiet, though, and the bossy Lady Russell is being well and truly bossed herself for the moment!"

"I wish I were there to see it!" Jo raised her eyes from the page to remark.

"To see what?" Jack demanded.

"Madge being well and truly bossed. She always managed to get round Nursie here, but Jem says the nuns are keeping her very much in order. Hooray! I'm all for it!" And with this unsisterly remark, she returned to the last of the letter.

"Of course, the boys will be baptized over here, and I

don't propose to invite you and Jack or the Bettanys to the party. Sorry; but it can't be done. However, if you like to come over in the spring and bring the girls with you and your own crowd, you'll be more than welcome. We ought to be thinking about coming some time in May, so if you came at Easter, you could have six weeks or a couple of months which would give you a good change, and allow the kids to be back at school at half-term.

"Now, Jo, don't bolt straight to the nearest phone, for the chances are that you'll catch no one. The girls are boarding at the Convent for the present, and I'm out most of the day. Ring, if ring you must, between six and nine in the evening, or before ten in the morning. I'm generally about then. I forget what time that will be in England. You'll have to work it out among you.

"Well, I think I've told you everything, and it's getting late and I'm sleepy. I'm giving this to a man I know who is flying home to-morrow, and he'll post it as soon as he lands, which will be as quick as anything else. I suppose you'll get it on Monday or Tuesday. If you want to be a nice kind sister, you might send Madge one of your famous epistles, telling her all about Sybil. She was rather inclined to be weepy at first because Sybs and David weren't with us to see their new brothers. However, she's got over that now, and is looking forward to the excitement of having them—with luck!—in the spring; Sybs, at any rate. Jack and Dick had better see what they think about David, and what his masters say about keeping him off school for a half-term or so. At his age, it may be best for himself to let him wait until we return.

"Now, good-bye, and take care of yourself. Madge sends fondest love to everyone, including Hilda and Nell, to whom you can break the news, and I wish I was a fly on the wall to hear their comments! Jem."

Jo finished this, and then sat folding it up and looking into the fire with unseeing eyes.

"What about it?" her husband asked.

"I simply can't get over the shock. It's the last thing I expected. I quite thought Ailie was to be the last of that

148

family. I'm very glad, though. Madge is a twin herself, so she *ought* to have twins! But I wish I could have been there." Jo suddenly jumped up.

"Where are you off to?"

"To find Sybs and tell her. Then I'm going to ring David up, and if Dick hasn't let him know, I will. After that, I suppose——Oh no; here they both are, so they shall hear first."

"What on earth——" Jack began; but the rest of his speech was forestalled by the opening of the door, and the entrance of the two Heads.

"Oh, you two!" Jo exclaimed. "I've got such news for you! You'll never guess in this world! Not if you try with both hands *and* your feet! Jack came over to tell me and to bring Jem's letter," she added. "Now then guess!"

Miss Annersley broke into laughter. "Then I shan't even attempt to try. You can tell us—and hurry up about it," she added.

Miss Wilson, however, made a shot. "It's in a letter from Sir Jem, then? Are they going to move the San to Canada—the Rockies or Labrador, for example?"

"No; it isn't anything like that. I'll tell you this much: it's a family affair, and has nothing to do with either the San or school."

"Madame agreed to be Corney's Matron-of-Honour after all?"

"No, it's not that. Besides, Corney was married three weeks ago. I'd have heard about that ages before this if it had come off."

"Then I give it up. Hurry up and break the news gently."

"O.K. Madge has had twin sons—a week old to-day!"

The pair stared speechlessly at her, and Miss Wilson collapsed limply into the nearest seat,

"And that's your idea of breaking news gently! I can't say I can congratulate you on it." Miss Annersley spoke sweetly. "And now, having done your best to pull our legs, suppose you go ahead and tell us what the news *really* is."

For reply, Jo turned to her husband. "Jack! *You* tell

them! They may believe you all right. And then I'll read them the first page of Jem's letter and perhaps they'll have managed to take it in after that!"

Miss Wilson chuckled. "Don't be so scathing, Jo. It's your own fault if Hilda thinks it a leg-pull. You've tried out a good many on us at one time or another." She paused, and eyed her ex-pupil gravely. "It really *is* true? Well, I'm breathless with surprise!"

"But no one hinted to us that anything was in the wind," Miss Annersley objected. "I'm sorry, Jo. I don't doubt your truth for a moment when you're serious. This was so unexpected I honestly thought you were trying to see just what we would swallow. However, I see that it *is* true. But why didn't any of you tell us what was expected?"

"Because none of us knew," Jack explained. "As a matter of fact, they weren't expected until January, but Madge seems to have hurried things up once more. She did with Sybil, you may remember. Jem also told me that Madge was afraid to let us know because she was certain Jo would worry herself sick about her. So they talked it over and decided to let it alone until the babies actually turned up, and then surprise us all. I may say they seem to have been completely successful in that last," he added with a wide grin. "If you two could only have seen your own faces when Jo sprang it on you! You looked like a couple of startled codfish!"

"This was so unexpected and amazing, we *both* thought you were trying it on Boys, you say? How nice! What does Sybil think of it?" said Miss Wilson

"She doesn't know yet. Lets send for her and tell her," Jo said with a sudden giggle. "I'll bet she'll be as floored as anyone."

Miss Wilson jumped up and went to the door. "Oh, Nancy Chester, Nancy!" she called; and they heard light feet returning. "Will you go and send Sybil Russell to the study, please? Tell her to hurry." Then she came back to her chair. "Sybil will be here in a moment."

Sure enough, Sybil appeared almost at once, a scared look on her face, as she tried to think of any reason why she should have been sent for like this. So far as she knew her conscience was reasonably clear for once. She slipped in, shut the door behind her, and made her curtsy. Then she saw her uncle, and raced across to him.

"Uncle Jack! Whatever are you here for?"

"Well, really! That's just the way your aunt greeted me. A more inhospitable pair I never met," he retorted. "You ask *her* what it's all about. She has some news for you."

"Sybs, come here!" Jo commanded, and Sybil went to her. "Do you remember when I told you that Mummy and Daddy wouldn't be home as soon as we thought?"

Sybil nodded. "You said it was because Dad was busy with some new work and they wanted to give Josette and Margot a chance to get really strong.—Oh, Auntie Jo. are they coming home for Christmas after all?"

Jo shook her head. "No my lamb; not till May at soonest. *But* I've just had a letter from your dad, and he suggests that when the Easter holidays come I should take you and my own crowd, and *perhaps* David, for a visit to Toronto. You see, old lady, they couldn't possibly come just now, or even for a month or two. Last Monday, two new little brothers arrived for you folk. How's that for a surprise?"

"Two *brothers*? You're sure it's brothers, Auntie, Jo? Really and truly? What are their names? Who are they like?"

"Kevin and Kester. Kevin is like your dad, and Kester seems to be like David."

"Oh, *wizard*! Absolutely super!"

Jo said hastily: "Wouldn't you like to tell Peggy and Bride and the others yourself? O.K. I thought you would. —Heavens! there's the bell! Jack, I must fly to set prep. Sybil, you buzz off and broadcast the news. You aren't going at once, Jack? The ferry doesn't leave till six, anyhow, so we can cross together." Then, as the excited Sybil curtsied and left the room, she turned to the Heads. "Forgive me, you two, but I honestly don't know if I'm standing on my heels or my head! Will you invite Jack and me to tea to talk this over with you? I'll be back directly!" Then she fled to dismiss her form after she had set their home-work, and told them the news, having sent Peggy to seek Sybil first. Lady Russell was the actual owner of the Chalet School, and the girls were all fond of her, so her sister felt it was their right to know what had happened.

"Twin boys?" Daphne gasped. "Oh, what a thrill after three girls! And now Madame has as many children as you and Mrs. Bettany."

Jo laughed. "She has indeed. I understand that Sir Jem is very pleased about that side of it."

"When shall we see the babies?" Frances asked eagerly.

"Oh, not before next spring, anyhow. She certainly won't want to cross the Atlantic with two tiny babies. I expect they'll be about six months old before she tackles that job. Now you must go and change, and I'm due for tea in the study. Mind those essays are ready for me on Thursday; and do think what you're saying before you commit it to paper and ink."

Jo nodded and escaped to the study, where she and her husband partook of a leisurely tea with the Heads and Mlle Lachennais, who was as excited about the news as anyone. When it was over, the visitors had to set off for the ferry, which was the last to the mainland in winter so they missed most of the thrills that pervaded the school when they heard that 'Madame' had managed to catch up with her brother and sister, and the Russells could say with the Bettanys and the Maynards—as Sybil did not fail to point out—"There's six of us!"

Chapter Fifteen

EILUNEDD'S PLOT

Eilunedd was alone in San, where she had been for three days with an unpleasant streaming cold. Matron always treated such things drastically, so Eilunedd had been whisked off to isolation, tucked into bed with hot-water bottles, Vick, and Thermogene, and well dosed with Matron's own remedy and hot milk. The cold had yielded to such treatment and she was feeling better, though still rather stuffed-up and achey. She had been allowed to get up half-way through the morning, and sit by the big log fire which brightened the room and the day. The weather had taken a wintry turn the day before, with a wet, blinding mist which had made everything feel clammy. Nurse, when she had taken away Eilunedd's tray after Mittagessen, had remarked with a shiver that it would not surprise her if they had sleet or snow before nightfall. She left then to minister to Frances Coleman, who was in the other room with a badly sprained ankle.

Eilunedd had plenty to read. Nurse had brought her knitting to her, and given her Patience cards and a couple of jigsaw puzzles; but she was bored with her book. She had knitted pretty steadily all the day before, and did not feel inclined to bother with it now. As for jigsaws, they would make her head ache, and she was not fond of Patience. Stretched out in the big armchair by the fire, she stared dreamily into the flames, and let her mind wander idly over the term's events. Quite the biggest, of course, was the arrival of the Russell twins. Eilunedd liked Lady Russell, and she was very glad for her. Thinking of the babies, her mind turned to their eldest sister, and she frowned

153

involuntarily. She had not given up her plan to get at Peggy Bettany through her young cousin; but Sybil had seemed uncommonly shy of her and sheered off from her on every occasion. Nor was there the least hope of doing it through Peggy's own sisters. Bride would never have listened to anything against Peggy; and Maeve was not a safe subject for anything of that kind, since she had an unholy trick of blurting out everything that came into her head.

Sitting there, the flames dancing and whispering to her, Eilunedd wondered what she could do. It was nearing the end of term, and if she meant to do anything about it, she must do it soon.

It was no use hoping to get Peggy into trouble for untidiness, for that young woman was tidy by nature and if she suddenly began losing her possessions there would be inquiries made. Neither could she see how to embroil her with other people. Peggy was close friends with two or three, such as Daphne Russell and Dickie Christy, and on friendly terms with the rest of her peers. She was an equable person, of sunshiny temperament, and the one bad quarrel of her schooldays had taken place some years before when they were all Junior Middles, and even then she had not really been to blame. On that occasion Eilunedd had sympathized with her. But now Peggy had been made Head Girl, the position Eilunedd herself had most coveted, and the silly girl was unable to see straight about it in her envy and disappointment.

"Surely I can think of *something*!" she thought, clasping her hands round her knees. "I've just got to get even with her for it! I *ought* to have been Head Girl this year. It's my last year, and she has another to come. She could have had it then, and it wouldn't have mattered. Oh, *why* couldn't the Heads have changed the rule for once and let me be Head?"

Try as she would, no ideas came to her, though she sat through the whole afternoon thinking. Nurse exclaimed when she brought the tea-tray at four, to find her sitting in the twilight. The fire had died down to a rosy mass, and the room was almost dark. Nurse set her tray down, switched on the light and pulled the curtains, and then told Eilunedd to throw a couple of logs on the fire while she pulled up the little table and set the tray on it.

"You shouldn't have let the fire go down like this," she scolded. "You're supposed to be in one temperature, and I'm sure this room has dropped since I left you. Yes," as she glanced at the wall thermometer, "it's barely sixty, and it's supposed to be sixty-five. You aren't really ill. Eilunedd, and you could quite well have made up the fire before this. Do you want to have a week in bed and miss the Christmas concert? What *were* you thinking about?"

"I'm sorry, Nurse," Eilunedd said, meekly enough; but she chalked this up as another bad mark against Peggy. If she hadn't been thinking so intently about her, she would have noticed the fire and attended to it, and then she wouldn't have been scolded.

Nurse sniffed and departed to see to Frances, and Eilunedd began on her tea, still thinking. Finally she had to give it up, for ideas refused to come. She opened her book and found the place, and picked up her knitting. It was a jumper in stocking-stitch, so she was able to read and knit together. The book was one of Jo Maynard's which, as it happened, she had never read—the first that lady had ever had published. Big girl as she was, Eilunedd found it interesting. Jo had a racy way of telling her story, and her characters were, on the whole, very true to life. The school in *Cecily Holds the Fort* was a day school, and the Chalet School was boarding, but here and there Eilunedd could see where the latter had given colour to the former. *Cecily*, the horoine, was a charming girl, and by no means too good to be true. Half-way through the book, she became embroiled with another girl, one *Sylvia Richardson*, who started a whispering campaign against her, and *Cecily* had some very unpleasant moments before she found out what was behind it all. *Cecily* in the story tackled *Sylvia*, and the result was that the quarrel was made up and the campaign stopped. Eilunedd read on breathlessly, noting points here and there which *Sylvia* had missed, and which

155

were the cause of her being found out. She read to the end, and then sat back triumphant. She had found her way at last! Just let her get out of San, and it would be odd if she couldn't contrive something that would give Peggy Bettany to think hard! She knew who would be the ideal person for her object too—Blossom Willoughby. No more heedless girl had ever entered the school. There was not an ounce of real harm in her, but she did things on an impulse without ever stopping to think before she did them. Eilunedd's eyes were sparkling as she thought out her plan. Nurse, glancing at her when she came to order her to bed, was startled by her flushed cheeks, and took her temperature, afraid that the girl had taken a fresh cold. However, Eilunedd was normal, so she decided that she must have been scorching her face over the fire, and let it go, even as she resolved to make sure the next morning that the temperature was staying normal.

Once she had gone with a pleasant "Good night; sleep well!" Eilunedd rolled over and began to think. She must have some sort of basis for her campaign, but that was not exactly easy to get. Peggy was, on the whole, a law-abiding creature, and so far no one but herself and Dickie knew anything about her lapse on the day of the great gale. Then the girl remembered the business of getting into the wrong train. She knew that Peggy was keeping up a pen-friendship with Nell Randolph, for the two had exchanged notes on their schools, and Peggy had entertained the Sixths with excerpts from the letters. The whole thing was supposed to have been a mistake, but was it?

Eilunedd knew that very little had been said to the Head Girl, and she also knew that the error had been the means of bringing Miss Annersley and her cousin together, so she supposed that was why Peggy had got off so lightly.

"Favouritism!" she thought bitterly. "That's all it is. Most likely that's why Peggy was chosen for Head Girl too, She's the staff pet! Well, I think I've got something there. I must go to work carefully, though. Pets get protection, and there's no point in having a row on my own account. This term is rotten enough without that."

She turned over again, and fell asleep at last, her mind finally made up. Two days later, she was pronounced free from infection and sent back into school with orders to keep out of draughts, and only to go out when the weather was fine, of which there seemed little likelihood at the moment. Nurse's prophecy had come true, and they were being treated to showers of sleet alternated with snow which lay for about a day and then melted into unpleasant slush. Games had to be cut out, as not one of the netball-courts or playing-pitches was in any state to be used, and the best they could do in the way of out-door excercise was a brisk short walk between showers. Naturally, Eilunedd was forbidden this, so the fresh air had no chance to blow away the cobwebs from her mind, and they clustered thick and fast.

Peggy had, by this time, forgotten Joan's warning at the begining of term. She was, as she remarked, up to her eyes in things just now. The Hobbies Club had decided to have a show of all the work they had done this term, and their collections besides. There was the Carol Concert which they were having this term instead of their usual Nativity Play. Peggy herself had a solo to sing, and the entire Sixth had undertaken to do programmes for it. Jo had booked the Parish Church Sunday Schoolroom for the performance, which must take place in Carnbach as crossing to the island in winter might not be possible. Everyone was anxious to make as much as possible for the children's Christmas party at the big Sanatorium in the mountains. Carnbach being very much off the beaten track. they could hardly hope for their usual big audience, even if the school-room would have held it. Therefore the Sixth had volunteered to paint programmes which they could sell for a shilling each. One or two really artistic people from the Fifths had been pressed into service, among them Polly Winterton, who was becoming known as one of Herr Laubach's most promising pupils.

Above and beyond all this, there was all the work a Head Girl was expected to do—and always lessons, though it must be admitted that during the last fortnight or three weeks of every Christmas term the school at large gave very little thought to such things. Peggy, it will therefore be seen, had her hands full, and as Eilunedd had made no sign as the term wore on, she had put the whole thing out of her head.

Eilunedd had been back in school for three days before she made any move. Then one afternoon when most of them, well wrapped up and attired in oilskins and wellingtons, were setting off for a walk, Miss Burn came hurrying into the Seniors' common-room.

"Oh, there you are, Eilunedd," she said. "I knew you weren't going out, so I told Miss Wilson I was sure you wouldn't mind keeping an eye on Blossom Willoughby and two or three more of her crowd who can't go out for various reasons. Blossom has toothache, and Meg Whyte has such awful chilblains, poor child, she's quite lame. There are one or two from Upper Third, and that new child, Shirley Westcott, from Lower. There's a Staff meeting this afternoon, and the rest of us have this walk. You can either bring the children in here, or have them in the Middles' common-room—please yourself. Thank you!" Miss Burn nodded brightly and vanished, and paused only to pick up her knitting, and then went off to the Middles' common-room, where she found most of the invalids sitting disconsolately round the fire. They brightened up a little as they saw her. When she was in the mood Eilunedd could tell the most enchanting stories from Welsh folklore, and they were all very bored, and, in the case of Blossom and little Shirley Westcott, in pain

"Oh, Eilunedd!" Meg exclaimed, getting to her feet and limping to meet the senior, "do come and tell us some of your lovely stories. It's such rotten weather, and we can't go out, and we're awfully browned-off."

"Well, not if you use slang like that," Eilunedd said. "Feet bad, Meg?" for she saw that Meg was wearing bedroom slippers.

"Simply ghastly! I can't even put my shoes on, my toes and heels are so swollen. Matey put ointment on them,

158

and they're all padded, so I just have to wear my bedders," Meg explained, limping back to her seat.

"Hard luck!" Eilunedd sat down in the chair some-one had pulled up for her, and unrolled her knitting. "I'll tell you one story, anyhow; more if there's time, perhaps. Get your work though."

They produced their work, and when they were all settled down, she began to tell them the story of Blodeuwedd, the Flower Maiden, who was created out of flowers for Prince Llew. Eilunedd knew and loved the tales in the Mabinogion, the book of Welsh folklore, and she had the Celt's musical voice which she used well. The seven or so Miseries sitting with her managed to forget most of their aches and pains as she talked, and when she ended her tale they pressed eagerly for another. She laughed and shook her head.

"There wouldn't be time The others will be back shortly We'll just talk for the short time left. Blossom, is your tooth bad?" as she saw the child twisting her face in an effort not to cry.

"It's pretty awful," Blossom said gruffly, blinking back the tears that at thirteen she was too proud to shed in public.

"Didn't Matey give you the chillie paste or anything?"

"Ye-es; but it hurts so to touch," Blossom explained.

"That hurt won't last more than a minute, and if you rub the paste on, it will ease the pain for quite a while. Don't be silly, Blossom! Bring it here to me and I'll do it for you,"

Blossom got up, produced her jar, and stood unwillingly while the senior gently rubbed the paste on to the swollen cheek. Her face was so tender that it took all her self-command to avoid crying out, but she managed it. though once again she had to blink hard before she faced the others.

"I wonder," said Meg thoughtfully, "if the Queen of Sheba ever had toothache? Wasn't she supposed to be absolutely lovely? But I suppose even she would look a guy with a swollen face."

"Or what if Cleopatra had chilblains like you?" retorted Blossom.

"Or Helen of Troy got a cold in the head and had a red

nose?" Anne Watson, who was suffering from a twisted ankle, chimed in. She giggled. "Do you think Menelaus or whoever it was would have wanted to run away with her then?"

"It was Paris, Prince of Troy," Eilunedd informed her. "Don't you kids *ever* listen to your lessons?"

"Oh, well, we did that last year," Meg said airily. "We're doing *As You Like It* for lit this. And Cleopatra wouldn't be likely to get chilblains, either. She lived in Egypt, and it's always warm there—or almost always anyhow!" She stooped down to rub a heel; then she stopped. "It's no use. I can't get at it, Matey's tied it up so."

"Just as well," Eilunedd said, laughing. "Leave your feet alone, Meg. The more you rub the worse they'll be."

"Bride Bettany once had a chilblain on the end of her nose," Blossom said reminiscently. The chillie paste was doing its good work already, and the pain in her face felt easier. "Poor Bride! She did look awful! And Matey couldn't pad up her nose very well."

"When was that?" Meg asked with interest.

"Years ago—before you came. It was when we were all kids in Upper Second. The next year Dr. Jem gave her tablets before the winter and she's not had any since. Dr. Jack says he's going to start me on them early next year. He looked at my feet when he came yesterday."

Eilunedd looked up from her knitting. "Hullo! Don't say you've got chilblains too! Toothache's enough for one person."

"One little one on my left little toe. It isn't bad, though, like Meg's. Hers are simply ghastly! Didn't he say he was going to start you too, Meg?"

Meg nodded. "Yes; but I wish someone had thought of it sooner."

"But you've never had chilblains like this before, have you? They wouldn't unless you did. There'd be no reason."

"Not since I was a wee kid. Oh, well, chilblains are pretty rotten, but I do think toothache is the worst pain of the lot."

"Earache is just as bad," Shirley said, from the depths

of the woolly scarf tied round her head. "It's just horrid the way it goes on and on! My cousin Althea, who's a bit younger'n me, gets it too. One year when they came to stay with us for Easter we *both* had it at once. Auntie said then she was afraid it was in the fam'ly 'cos she used to get it when she was a little girl."

"Is your cousin ever coming here?" Anne demanded.

"Oh no," Shirley's brown eyes grew big and wide. "I wanted her to but she's gone to another school with her big cousin, at Branscombe Park, near Ludlow. She's a big girl, and looks after Althea. She isn't my cousin at all," she added.

Blossom remembered something. "Branscombe Park? Why, that's where that girl Peggy Bettany met when they got lost on the train coming here goes to school. Peggy writes to her, and so does she,"she added vaguely.

Shirley forgot her earache and nodded vigorously. "I know. Althea my cousin *sometimes* writes to me, and she told me Nell told her all about meeting Peggy and the others on the train. Wasn't it a *funny* mistake they made?" she added, dissolving into giggles.

"Very funny!" Eilunedd replied drily. "Not in the least like Peggy Bettany. She's a careful soul as a rule, and *doesn't* make silly mistakes like that. It almost makes one think—— But no; that wouldn't be like Peggy, either."

"What do you mean?" Blossom asked, suddenly becoming alert.

"Nothing in the world. Just that while some girls might have done it on purpose just to see what would happen, Peggy, as I've said, is the last person on earth to think of such a thing. *You* would, though, Blossom!" she added, laughing. "I don't advise you to try, however."

"No," Blossom agreed. "I get into too many rows for anyone to let me off if I did a thing like that. Peggy never has—got into rows."

"Ah, well, she's older than you. And then again, there's a lot to be said for being Lady Russell's niece too," Eilunedd replied as she gathered up her work, for her quick ear had caught the sound of voices, and she knew that the others were returning. "You'd better all stay here until tea-time," she said, as she went to the door. "It must be nearly that now. Blossom, if that tooth aches badly again, don't be a little owl, but use the chillie paste. It's worth it, isn't it?"

Blossom, completely diverted by this, nodded slowly. "Yes; it is," she owned honestly. "The ache's nearly gone. I just know it's there, but that's all. Still I *s'pose* I'd better not take jam for tea."

"Not if you don't want it again in full force," Eilunedd agreed, making her escape, quite satisfied with the afternoon's work. She knew that she had succeeded in implanting an idea into the minds of the younger girls. Some of them might forget, but it was pretty safe to say that one or two wouldn't, and the next time Peggy hauled them over the coals for some sin or other they would remember, and say something about it to the rest of their crew.

This, as it happened, occurred the very next day when Blossom herself, freed from her toothache through taking Eilunedd advice and applying the chillie paste properly, celebrated the event by 'saucing' Peggy when called to order for sliding down the bannisters.

Peggy, hurrying from one lesson to another, had to go past the stairs the school used, and glancing up, saw Blossom fling a leg across the rail, and prepare to slide down.

"Blossom Willoughby! Come down at once!" she said peremptorily. Whether Blossom was startled into it or not, no one ever knew. The fact remains that in one sense she obeyed Peggy quite literally. She *did* come down—down the bannister—and with such speed that she was unable to brake as she neared the foot, and ended in a heap on the floor at the righteously indignant Head Girl's feet. Peggy dropped her book and stooped over her to demand anxiously if she were hurt.

Blossom, a hardy young thing took, harder knocks than this without whimpering. She gathered herself together, looked up at the anxious Peggy with sea-blue eyes full of wickedness, and said sweetly: "Not hurt at all; but I'll bet you think it's a lot more than I deserve."

Peggy stiffened. "That will do," she said. "Stand up, please."

Blossom got to her feet, eyeing the Head Girl warily. The imp that lived within her had taken full possession for the moment; all the same, she was not anxious to get a Head's report. She decided, unfortunately for everyone that Peggy could take a little more.

"And what next?" she asked, as pertly as she dared.

"*Next*, you may go and report yourself in the study," Peggy replied, after looking her up and down with the effect that such a creature was almost beneath her notice.

"Oh, *blow!*" Now the worst had happened, Blossom decided she might as well be hung for a sheep as a lamb. "It was just a slide."

"Breaking a rule," Peggy reminded her, "Also being rude to me."

"You're not such a frightfully important person as all that," the offender muttered; but Peggy was meant to hear, and she heard.

"I think your go of toothache must have gone to your head," she observed. "Go and do as I tell you, please, and don't answer me again."

"What shall I say?" Blossom sounded a little subdued. She had already had one Head's report this term. To have a *second* in the same term was an almost unheard-of thing, for consequences were, as a rule, too shattering to be risked twice in three or four months.

"You may tell whoever is there that you have been sent for breaking rules and impertinence and defiance, "Peggy told her.

The imp was quelled by this time. Blossom took a step forward. "Oh, please, Peggy, if I apologize—I really do mean it—and—and write dozens of lines instead, won't you let me off the report?" she begged.

"You heard what I said?" was all Peggy vouchsafed.

Her repentance forgotten, Blossom flung away. "I think you're *mean*, Peggy Bettany!" she choked. "You jolly well never get into a row yourself; but you get other

163

people! P'raps, though, if everyone knew, you aren't so awfully good as all that, yourself!"

Peggy took a stride after her, and caught her by the shoulder, looking down at her with puzzled blue eyes. "You aren't well," she said. "Here; wait!" And, picking up her books, she hastily tore a sheet out of her jotting-pad, scribbled a few words on it, then folded it, and gave it to Blossom. "Take that to Matron before you do anything else," she ordered. "Now hop! I'm sick of you!"

Blossom took it, and turned unwillingly to mount the stairs again in search of Matron. Even in her present mood she dared not disobey the Head Girl and so bring extra trouble on herself. A Head's report when you reported yourself was quite bad enough. If a prefect or a mistress reported you, it was ten times worse. Just the same, she would have given worlds to know what Peggy had said to Matron in that note. And she would have given an entire universe not to have spoken so rudely to Peggy. Why on earth had she made things so much worse for herself?

Matron read the note, gave her a look which sent all her courage down into her shoes, and then said: "You'd better see what a little extra bed will do for you. Come here and let me look at your mouth."

Blossom obeyed, and Matron looked searchingly into her wide open mouth before she said briskly: "H'm! One tooth that will have to come out, or I'm much mistaken, and two to be filled. You'll visit the dentist tomorrow, and we'll see what he can do for you. Now be off to bed with you, and don't let me have any trouble."

Blossom scuttled off, and was into bed in short order. Nor did she find it very cheerful, lying there all by herself in the big room, her curtains drawn, and nothing to read but her Bible, which she didn't feel inclined to touch at the moment. Tea consisted of a bowl of bread-and-milk and she was never fond of bread-and-milk, and when supper brought the same thing, she would have protested if she dared: but she didn't dare. She seemed to have got off that Head's report, but she had to face the dentist, which was almost as bad. Peggy really had been mean about it all! She never stopped to think that Matron would probably have insisted on the visit without Peggy to spur her on, but most unfairly blamed the whole thing on the Head Girl.

"It's all very well," she thought sulkily, "but Peggy always behaves as if she'd never done a single wrong thing in her life, and I'll bet she has—dozens of them!" And then, all unbidden, Eilunedd's queer remarks of the day before rose in her mind, and she began to wonder. Could Peggy really have done the whole thing on purpose? And had she really escaped trouble because she was Lady Russell's niece and a pet of the two Head's? Blossom worried over this until she fell asleep, and still had not solved it. Part of her said it was all nonsense; part of her wondered if it could be really true, and said that if it was it was too jolly unfair for anything. She set off with Matron and five other unhappy beings next morning, bound for Cardiff and the dentist, with the puzzle still a puzzle. Nor, when they returned, herself very furious, for the drilling of the teeth had been a most painful thing, and she still had an aftermath of aching bothering her, was she any surer which she truly believed.

Chapter Sixteen

CONSEQUENCES

Blossom remained in her bewildered state for the rest of the week and it made her thoroughly unlike herself. Unluckily, Peggy fell foul of two or three more folk in the same form, and the malcontents came together to discuss the state of affairs with vim.

"It's all very well the prees behaving as if they'd never been anything but the goodest little girls all their lives," Mayna Unsworth grumbled. "I'll bet when they were our age they did a lot of worse things than us! I'm sick of being forever hauled up for the least thing!"

"Well, *you* asked for it, playing that silly trick with a bucket of water!" Hilary Wilson growled. "It's all very well in summer, but to do a mad thing like that in winter is the outside edge!"

One or two of the others agreed with her. A careless housemaid had left a bucket in the Splasheries just before Upper Fourth went trooping in to wash their hands after gym. During the previous term, some of them had discovered that if you swing a toy bucket containing a little water round and round fast enough, the water stays where it is. Some demon had prompted Mayna to catch up Olwen's bucket, half fill it at the tap, and try the effect of swinging round with it herself. She had been spinning dizzily in the middle of the floor while the rest watched her with a fearful joy, when Dickie Christy bounced in to demand what all the noise was about. Mayna was at the top of her spin—plus bucket—and the result was that in the sudden shock she stopped dead and toppled over, while the bucket went flying into a corner, mercifully without hitting anyone, but liberally spraying those near with chilly water. Dickie had been righteously angry, and Mayna had received a sharp rebuke coupled with the loss of her Saturday night fun. As the Sixth were to be hostesses, and producing 'Scenes from *Little Women*', Mayna smarted. While the rest were enjoying the doings of *the Marches* and their friends, she would be sitting in the linen room, hemming the long side of a sheet; and Mayna loved plain sewing no more than most youngsters of thirteen do.

Isobel Drew, a promising twelve-year-old who was six months below the average age of the form, but made up for that with original sin, sighed deeply. "Well, all I've got to say is that if the prees expect us to think they were all little angels when they were our age, they've got another think coming!" she declared.

"How do you mean?" Blossom asked curiously.

"Why, of course they couldn't! If they had, they'd never be able to catch us out as they do." Isobel spoke feelingly. The night before, she had occupied herself between tea and prep in pouring a modicum of the olive oil with which she had to wash her face in winter into the inkwells in her form-room, with the result that no one was able to write properly.

The others giggled reminiscently.

"Wasn't Peggy mad!" Hilary said with a chuckle.

"That part of it was funny all right. But she needn't have gone and guessed what was wrong. And if she did, she *jolly* well needn't have gone to Matey about it!" Isobel spoke with a good deal of bitterness, for she, too, had lost her Saturday night, only in her case Matron had ordered bed at seven, which, so Isobel thought, was adding insult to injury. "You bet Peggy's done that sort of thing, or she couldn't have guessed *what* I'd put in. Anyhow, I don't know how she hit on me for it at all."

"That was your own fault," they told her. "When Peggy said, 'Who's been messing about with the ink?' you went crimson, so of course she guessed it was you."

"She's not *daft*, even if she is being horridly sticky this term," Meg Whyte added. "You always give yourself away by going red, Isobel."

"Well, I can't *help* it!" Isobel spoke defensively.

"Then don't grouch because you're caught out." This was Blossom. "All the same," she went on in injured tones, "I don't see why Peggy should put on such airs. After all, look what she did at the beginning of term?"

"What *do* you mean?" Hilary opened big eyes at her.

"Why, coming back a day late—and when she had two new girls with her as well as young Maeve."

"That was an accident," Hilary protested.

"Accident my foot! They've come by that train before and made no mistake. Why should it happen this term? And if you come to that," Blossom went on, the yeast of Eilunedd's hints working within her, "why did she get off like that. She didn't get into any sort of row."

"How do *you* know that?" The demand came in a chorus.

Blossom gave them a pitying smile. "Well, if she had,

do you asses *really* think she'd have been made Head Girl the very next minute? Use your sense—if you've got any!"

"Or if she did," she went on, the memory of her wrongs surging up and obliterating any common sense she had left, "then it was just favouritism of the Heads, and that's beastly unfair."

"But," suggested Hilary, who usually kept her head better than most of them, "if they hadn't chosen Peggy, who could they have chosen? Joan is heaps the best for games, and Dickie Christy was new last term, and I don't think any of the others could have taken it on."

"There was Eilunedd, wasn't there?" Blossom demanded.

"She's in Special Sixth, and they don't *be* prefects," someone pointed out.

Blossom swept this aside. "That's all rot. They used to. Daisy Venables was Special Sixth when she was Head —and so was Robin Humphries. It only ended after that girl Marilyn what's-her-name. Something went wrong then, and Bill and the Abbess said after that that Special Sixth had too much work or something, so they'd better be left out. But Eilunedd isn't doing any exams or music or art and things like that. And she *was* a pree last year. Peggy wasn't even a sub!"

"No; that's true; she wasn't," Hilary agreed. Then she glanced at her watch and gave a positive squeak of horror. "I *say*! It's nearly ten past two! We can't ever have heard the bell, and it's Miss Stephens for geog! Come on, you folks!"

With cries of dismay, they snatched their hooded cloaks, pulling them on as they ran, and bolted for the geography room, where the reception they got from an excusably angry Miss Stephens did nothing to calm their feelings. In their excitement, none of them had seen a small nine-year-old slip out of the Splashery just before Hilary made her dramatic announcement; but small Judy Willoughby, Blossom's sister, had heard enough to give her something to discuss with her own special chums, and by the time the

Saturday had come, it was all over the Junior school that Peggy Bettany had made the mistake about the train on purpose, only the Heads let her off because of her Auntie Madge, and really she oughtn't to be Head Girl any more than anyone—to quote little Janice Chester, youngest sister of Nancy Chester, the prefect of Five A.

From this, it was just a step to defiance of her, because, as Della Armstrong of Lower Fourth pointed out, if she had no right to be Head Girl, then it was just as if she wasn't; which fine example of muddled thinking pleased the worst imps among them all.

Of course, quite a number refused to believe a word of it. Both Len and Con Maynard stood up manfully for Peggy, and so did her own small sister Maeve, as well as Mary-Lou Trelawney, and that young person's special chums. Most of the others were divided, and the result was that there was an uneasy atmosphere in the school. Oddly enough, the rumour never reached the higher forms, though the prefects sensed something wrong, but they were puzzled to say what it was.

"There's a kind of defiant feeling when you're handling some of those youngers," Nina Williams said, towards the end of the next week. "What it is, I'd be puzzled to say, but it's there all right."

Dickie put down the pencil with which she had been tracing the outlines of a map of India. "I don't believe in sounding their little pals as a rule," she said slowly, "but I caught Cherry at home last night, and tried to get something out of her. The kid went completely clam-like on me, and wouldn't say a word—except that she didn't believe it, and that was that. It was all I could get out of her, anyhow."

"It'll be some nonsense or other," Nita Eltringham said scornfully.

"But could you put your finger on any one thing and say: 'That's it'?" Nina demanded with point.

Nita shook her head. "No; it's more of an atmosphere than anything concrete. Nancy Chester told me some weird tale she'd got out of young Janice, but it was such a garbled affair that I didn't bother much about it. Something to do with Peggy and that weird journey of theirs when we came back to school. That's all I know."

The door opened, and the three girls looked round guiltily. However, it was only Judy Rose and Barbara Henschell who came in. Judy was looking annoyed, and Barbara was plainly bewildered.

"Hello!" Dickie said cheerfully. "Who's eaten your pet canary, Judy?"

"It's those brats of Lower Thirds," Judy replied stormily. "I'd like to tie the lot in a bag and drop them into the sea off Brandon Mawr! Little beasts!"

"What have they been doing?" Nina demanded.

"Oh, the usual thing—cheeking folk as far as they dare. When one ticks them off and sends them to their own room, they go, of course; but it's very much as if they only did it because they chose to. And Mary-Lou and Phil Craven have been having a row and very nearly came to blows. In fact, they were hanging on to each other, and only parted when I grabbed a shoulder of each and shook them as hard as I could."

"You're not supposed to shake them" Nita said. "What were they rowing about?"

"Haven't the foggiest! Bab came along and grabbed Mary-Lou and marched her off to her form-room while I dealt with young Phil. Not that I got any sort of information out of her. All she would say was, 'It's a private matter, so I can't tell you.' Finally, I docked her Saturday night, and told her if it occurred again she could take a Head's report. That rather sobered her down, thank heaven!"

"What about our one and only Mary-Lou?" Nina asked Barbara.

"More or less the same thing—except that she coolly informed me that if Phil Craven didn't stop saying things she'd box her ears."

"Good heavens! How ferocious!" Nina began to laugh. "What *can* Phil Craven have been saying to get Mary-Lou's dander up like that?"

"I couldn't tell you. She flatly refused to say anything more. I adopted Judy's tactics, and told her the next time she made a scene like that she'd find herself in the study with a Head's report. I can't say she seemed to mind awfully much. She simply said that Phil could mind what she was saying, or she'd be sorry! I gave it up after that. You know," Barbara went on earnestly, "Mary-Lou was certainly defiant but it was a—a *nice* defiance."

"There ain't no such animile," Nina murmured; while Dickie stared and remarked: "That's a contradiction in terms. What are you getting at?"

"Well, I mean it!" Barbara still looked bewildered, but she stuck to her guns. "When some of those kids talk like that it just makes me see red; but Mary-Lou wasn't *rude* about it—she was simply stating a fact. There's a difference, you know."

Nita nodded. "I see what you mean. All the same, they can't be allowed to fight like schoolboys. Thank goodness there's only another ten days of term to go, and this afternoon we start in on real hard work on the concert. That ought to occupy the things they're pleased to call their minds, and give *us* a little peace.

Judy flopped into the nearest chair. "It's all very well, but unless we clear things up this term, will this sort of thing go on next? That's what I want to know!"

"What's what you want to know?" a fresh voice asked, as Joan Sandys came in and tossed her armful of books down on the table. "Oh, I'm tired! I've had a regular doing with Bill. Thank goodness that finishes science for this term, anyhow!" She stretched out her foot and hooked a chair to her and sat down. "Tell me what's wrong with you, Judy." But at Judy's account of Mary-Lou and Phil Craven, she sat up alertly. "Oh! And you couldn't get any idea what it was all about?"

"Not a word. As Dickie says, Phil went clamlike on me and wouldn't say a thing. And Mary-Lou seems to have done the same thing with Bab."

Joan dug her hands into her blazer pockets and frowned at the toes of her shoes. "H'm! I *wonder*!"

"What do you wonder?" Nita demanded. "Have you any idea what it's all about? If so, for goodness' sake tell us, and then perhaps we can do something about it. There's certainly something up with that crowd."

Joan got up and shook out her skirt. "I can't do anything about it for the moment. I must do some 'teckery. If it's what I think it is, then *you* ought to know about it. Dick.' Her brown eyes went to Dickie. "Remember what we said at the beginning of term?"

Dickie thought. "We said such a lot," she complained. "I—— *Oh*!" She looked straight at Joan. "I think I see what you're getting at now. But that's almost three months ago, and this is the first I've seen of anything that could be in that line."

"What *is* all this in aid of?" Nina demanded. "Why are you two all cryptic and mysterious? *What* did you say at the beginning of term?"

"You'll have to wait," Joan said blandly. "I told you I'd have to do a spot of sleuth-hound. If it's what I think it is, then all I've got to say is that someone is a complete idiot. However, I'll let you know as soon as I can. Hello! Here comes someone else."

The door opened, and six or seven more girls, headed by Peggy, came in: and a very angry Peggy she was. Her blue eyes glowed with fire, and her pretty mouth was set in a straight line.

"Look here," she said, going straight to the point before she had even unloaded herself of her books, "can any of you tell me what is at the bottom of all this defiance and impudence from the kids?"

"Joan seems to think she has an idea," Nina said. "She's talking mysteriously of being a female Sexton Blake and letting us know the results as soon as possible. Who's been doing or saying what to you?"

"Oh, just the usual thing. I told three or four of them who were hanging about the corridor to hurry up and get ready for Mittagessen; and then, if you please, that brat Phil Craven said, 'I'll suit myself, thank you. I'll be in plenty of time.' I could have wrung her neck! That gang she hunts with were all there, and they all giggled. I dealt out conduct marks all round with an extra two for Phil to give her something to think about, but they didn't seem unduly upset."

"Phil should have been upset all right," Judy remarked. "She's been docked of her Saturday already—I saw to that myself just now—so if you've given her three conduct marks, that means she goes to her form-mistress. I should say Miss Phil was very much in the soup."

"Well, this sort of thing has got to *stop*! If I have much more of it I shall report the lot to Miss Annersley for general insubordination."

The prefects looked grave.

"I say, you don't want to do that if we can tackle them any other way," Judy said quickly. "It's the same thing as saying that we can't do our own work—a confession of incapacity."

"I know; but what else can I do? If this sort of thing goes on, it's going to ruin the feeling in the school—or in the lower part of it, anyhow. We can't have that."

"Mrs. Maynard is coming this afternoon, isn't she?" Nina asked. "Well, why don't you tell her and see what she says? She seems to have had a good many weird things to deal with when *she* was Head Girl. And, thank goodness, she won't tell what to the Heads unless it's absolutely necessary. Meantime, Joan and Dickie can get on with their sleuthing, and perhaps they'll be able to find out what is at the back of it all."

Peggy thought this over. It was good advice, she knew; but she was still very angry. Phil's manner had been almost unbearably insolent, and though she was a sweet-tempered girl, Peggy Bettany had a strong sense of dignity which Phil had outraged.

Daphne Russell, who had come into the room with her, knew this. No more than the rest did she want to take their latest problem to the Heads if they could deal with it themselves, so she took a hand.

"Didn't Jo help to deal with some other things even after she had left school?" she inquired of the room at large.

"Dozens of times," Peggy replied. "There was all the fuss with Eustacia Benson. And then they had some choice Middles in her time—Corney Flower, who was married in October, and Evadne Lannis, and Elsie Carr, and a whole crowd like that. And you remember Miss Linton——"

"Seeing she only left last term, we haven't had much time to forget her," Nita said sweetly. "What about her? Don't tell me she was ever a sickening Middle, for I shan't believe it."

"She was *not*! But her young sister Joyce was the outside of enough! Though I believe Mary Burnett was Head Girl that term. On the whole, Nina, I think yours is a good plan. I'll try to get Auntie Jo alone when she comes and—— Oh, I've had a brain-wave! Let's ask her to tea with us! Who's got any tuck left? I've half a seed cake, and some chocolate biscuits, and one pot of honey."

"I've got some of my birthday cake left," Frances replied.

"I believe there's the fag-end of a jar of blackberry jelly in my box," Nina contributed. "Anyone else got anything?"

It was too near the end of term, however, and beyond some oddments of jam, no one else could make a contribution. Still, when they had assembled the lot, they decided that Jo being Jo would not turn up her nose at the feast, and Peggy was deputed to invite her to tea in the prefects' room after the carol practice, when they proposed to lay their troubles before her and ask her advice.

When Jo arrived, she was promptly cornered by her eldest niece, and cheerfully agreed to come to tea with them.

"Though I mayn't be able to help you in the least," she pointed out. "Still, you can get your troubles off your chests, and that will be a relief, at any rate. What

174

reason have you given the Heads for your tea-party, by the way?"

Peggy looked startled. "Mercy! We were all so revved up we never thought of it! I'd better go and ask leave at once."

"Well, it might be a good idea," Jo assented.

Miss Annersley laughed when Peggy politely asked if they might have Mrs. Maynard to tea with them after carol practice, and gave her consent at once.

"I'm sure she'll enjoy it. Your aunt is still a schoolgirl in spots, Peggy. How are you folk off for food?"

"We've some cake and remnants of jam," Peggy admitted. "It isn't much, but Auntie Jo won't mind that."

"I'm certain she won't! However, Cook has made paris buns for me, so she can send you a plateful, and some Welsh cakes as well."

"Oh, thank you, Miss Annersley. That will be splendid!"

Peggy curtsied and withdrew, and the Head was left to smile to herself. "I suppose they mean to ask Jo's advice about the conduct of those young imps in the Fourth and Lower School," she mused. "I'll be glad if they can deal with it without coming to us. It would make it a very serious matter if we had to deal with it."

The carol practice went well under the guidance of Mr. Denny, the school's capable if eccentric singing-master. The girls all loved their singing-lessons; all the same, the prefects were very glad for once when the hour's practice came to an end and they were at liberty to stream off to their own quarters and prepare tea for their visitor. The rest of the school had three-quarters of an hour's prep, mostly in charge of various members of the staff. Dickie and Joan, however, disappeared in the direction of the form-rooms, leaving the others to see to tea. Nor did they turn up again until the visitor had been seated in state near the fire and supplied with a cup of tea and one of Cook's delectable Welsh cakes. Then they arrived, looking rather serious but quite pleased with themselves.

"There's a smugness about you two that tells me you

have news," Jo remarked as she surveyed them. "Come on and tell us the latest."

"Take your tea first," Peggy said practically, from behind the big tea-urn which she was manipulating. She handed over their cups, and then sat back with her own tea.

"Before you begin," Jo said, demolishing the last of her cake and helping herself to another, "I'd like to know the trouble first. Go ahead and tell me, and don't all talk at once."

Between them, they told her what had been happening during the last week or two, and she frowned as she listened. Then she turned to Joan and Dickie.

"Have you two found out anything? I may as well have the whole thing clear before I say anything."

Joan nodded, looking grave. "Well, it's as we thought. Eilunedd began it all."

"Eilunedd? But, bless me, she's a senior—was a prefect last year, wasn't she?" Jo exlaimed.

"That's part of the trouble, we think. She's the only one of that lot that didn't expect to go into Special Sixth, and if she hadn't she would have naturally been Head Girl. Her Dad decided she ought to be specializing, however, so she moved up, and you know what happened when Marilyn Evans was Head, don't you?" Joan demanded. After that a rule was made that no Special Sixth might be Head Girl. So instead of Eilunedd, it was Peggy—and she's done jolly well," she added generously. "Just the same, Eilunedd's queer, and she blames Peg because she wasn't Head Girl. I think—and so does Dick—that she's started this ramp to make things so awkward for Peg that the Head will think she's too inexperienced to manage and have to call Eilunedd in to take on the job. There isn't one of *us* who would like to take it on!"

A murmur of assent ran round the table at this.

Jo looked startled.

"But look here," she objected, "how do you know all this?"

"Well," Joan said slowly, "it seemed to be Blossom

Willoughby who was the leader in all this, so we asked for her from prep and questioned her."

"You know what Blossom is!" Dickie took a hand. "She can't keep a thing to herself. We took her to our own common-room, and then Joan said: 'What has Eilunedd been saying to you kids about Peggy Bettany?' Blossom went red, but Joan told her she could either tell us or go to the Heads, so she hadn't much choice."

"I'll say she hadn't," Jo agreed. "Well, what did she tell you?"

Very soberly, the pair told the others about Eilunedd's hints, and as she listened, Peggy flushed, and her blue eyes glowed with anger. Only Daphne's hand, gripping her arm firmly, kept her in her seat. Jo was watching her, too, and when Dickie uttered the last sentence, she leapt into the breach, giving her niece no time to voice the rage that was mounting in her.

"Yes. Well, Eilunedd is a silly young ass who certainly hasn't attempted to think things out, or she'd have known that the fact that Peg as Madame's niece would only have made things a lot worse for her if anyone had had any reason to think there was anything fishy about that train business. I know," she added feelingly, "that when *I* was at school and caught out—and I don't mind telling you at this late date that it happened more than once— I caught it a good deal hotter than anyone else, just *because* I happened to be her sister. So Eilunedd must have taken leave of her senses to suggest such a thing. As for the kids, most of them haven't any brains to speak of— their heads are filled with a porridgy mush to take their place! Really, Peg, I know it's horribly annoying, but it's so silly that it's beneath your dignity to pay any attention to it. Now let me think—and don't talk, any of you."

This effectually closed everyone's mouth—and a good many people had been burning to say what they thought. Jo kept them in suspense for a good five minutes. Then she nodded, and her black eyes lighted up with wickedness.

"All right! I've got it! You folk can leave Eilunedd

to me: I'll deal with her. As for the little idiots, I propose you call a meeting and tell them the exact facts. Peggy had better keep out of it, by the way, but one of you others can do it. You might point out that in any case, so long as she was appointed by the Heads, she is the Head Girl and they are asking for trouble if they get up against her." Then she asked anxiously, "I hope my pair and Mary-Lou aren't in it?"

"Not they!" Judy told her. "In fact, Mary-Lou has been in bad trouble to-day for beginning a stand-up fight with Phil Craven on the subject.

"Very well, then." Jo passed up her cup for more tea. "Do as I said and leave Eilunedd to me. You don't want to take a thing of this kind to the Heads if you can help it. They'd be bound to take notice of it and it might become serious if that happened. Not," she added, as she received her full cup, "—thanks, Peggy!—that I believe for one moment that they know nothing about it. I'll bet any money they *do*. But they won't want to interfere if you folk can grapple with it." She drained her cup, refused the last sliver of seed-cake, and stood up. "Anyone know where I'm likely to find Eilunedd? In the common-room? Good! I must have a word or two with her, and see Len and Con, and then I'll have to run for it, or I'll miss the ferry. Good-bye till Monday."

"Auntie Jo, what are you going to do?" Peggy demanded suddenly.

Jo made a face at her. "Wouldn't you like to know! I'll give you all one hint. Isn't it a splendid thing that it's turned so mild after all the stormy weather we've been having? Bye-bye!" And she departed, leaving them staring and wondering what on earth she meant.

Chapter Seventeen

HAPPY ENDING

The next day, the prefects followed Jo's advice. Dickie, as Second Prefect, called a meeting of all forms between the Kindergarten, who knew nothing about the matter, and Five C, to take place between tea and prep. The rest of the prefects agreed to be there to back her up, though they told Peggy to have some important engagement which she was unable to break. As it happened, Miss Wilson—*had* Jo passed the word to her?—summoned the Head Girl to her own preserves for a reason not stated, to Peggy departed with an easy conscience, while the rest rather nervously made their plans.

"I wish to goodness we could get some outside proof that Peggy was not to blame for being in the wrong part of the train," Dickie said, as she glanced down her notes.

As if in answer to this, there came a tap at the door, and when someone opened it, there stood a complete stranger—a long-legged girl with wide brown eyes, who said: "Oh, I'm Nell Randolph. My uncle, Commander Mordaunt, came to see your Head, Miss Annersley, on business—they're cousins—and she sent me here to find Peggy Bettany. But," she added, casting a glance round the room, "she isn't here. Can you tell me where I can find her?"

"She's with our other Head, Miss Wilson," Dickie said.

She was interrupted by Daphne. "Dick! The outside proof you wanted. Here it is!" She turned to Nell, who was staring at her in amazement. "Are you the girl she met on the train when they went to Gloucester by mistake? But I know you are. Well, then, you can help us."

Dickie smote on the table. "Of course she can! Come in and sit down, Nell, and we'll tell you what we want.

179

It's this way, you see." And she explained as briefly as she could.

Nell nodded thoughtfully when she had finished. "Aren't juniors little *asses*? I can help all right! There was nothing fishy about *that* business, I can tell you! I thought Peggy was going crackers when she understood what had happened! Now tell me what you want me to do. Poor old Peggy! I'd like to scrag the little brute that got the idea!"

Dickie had carefully avoided mentioning about Eilunedd, merely saying that one of the Junior Middles had started the idea, and passed it round to the others, so Nell spoke in all innocence. The prefects had no notion of giving the Senior away, so they hurried to explain the general idea, and Nell fell in with it at once.

"I see. Well, suppose you just say I've something to tell them, and let me loose on them! When I've finished, you can rub it in while I come back here to wait for Peggy. How'll that do?"

"Jolly good!" Dickie said appreciatively. "They'll listen all right to a stranger, and then we can hoe in. What's the time, anyone? Ten to five? Then some of you go and do sheepdog. We'll come along in ten minutes from now."

Daphne, Judy, Nita and Barbara departed to march the younger girls into Hall, and the rest sat chatting with the lively Nell, who gave them a vivid account of her meeting with Peggy's party, until Nina glanced at the clock and jumped up, exclaiming, "Five o'clock!"

"Come on," Dickie said, leading the way. "Mind your landmarks as you go, so that you can get back. Or shall someone come with you?"

"I can find my way all right, thank you," Nell answered, as she followed the Second Prefect down the corridor, along another, down the stairs, through a little passage, and so into the entrance hall where, through the open doors, they could see the lower portion of the school sitting in Hall, all chattering and giggling.

Dickie frowned blackly at this sign of indiscipline, but

180

she said nothing. She made for the dais, Nell following, and the rest of the Chalet School prefects going to their usual seats. When she got there, Dickie struck the bell on the mistress's lectern, and the chatter died down by degrees.

The Second Prefect believed in going straight to the point, and she certainly did so on this occasion. She waited until there was absolute silence, and the girls were all looking at her—those of them who were not looking with wild curiosity at Nell—and then she spoke.

"This is Nell Randolph," she said, waving her hand at Nell, who blushed darkly red, though she lifted her head, and looked at them with a meditative interest that somehow affected more than one unpleasantly. "She has something important to say to you all."

Having made her announcement, Dickie sat down, and Nell stood forward.

"Good evening," she said. "I expect you wonder what a total stranger can have to say to you. I've been told that all sorts of silly, garbled stories about what happened to the Bettanys and the Wintertons on their way to school at the beginning of term are going round among you. As I was there and saw most of it, I thought it would be as well to tell you the whole thing. There's nothing to be gained by listening to lies and believing in them, is there?"

At this bland question, two or three people wriggled and went red, and Lala Winterton suddenly looked at the stranger with recognition in her eyes. She straightened up in her seat, though she said nothing. As for Mary-Lou and her gang, who were together as usual, they looked painfully smug, for they, at least, had not believed the tales, and had said so, as we have seen.

Now that she had taken the plunge, Nell was her own man. Leaning one arm on the lectern, she told the story of how Peggy and the rest had nearly missed the train altogether, and the well meaning porter had lifted Maeve into the compartment, and helped to bundle in the rest.

"They simply hadn't any choice," Nell said, while the

Lower School sat in deathly silence. "That man just shot them in, one after the other, with their cases, and slammed the door on them as the train was moving. It was chock-a-block, so they had to park in the corridor where I was having to stand too. It wasn't until Peggy realized that they ought to have gone the other way, and I heard her saying it to the others and explained, that any of them knew what had happened." Suddenly she shook with laughter. "In all my life I've never seen anyone look more utterly appalled than Peggy did at that moment! I quite thought she was going to pull the communication cord, and that would have done no one any good, for we were miles past the place where the train—er—separates. It might only have meant a row and her father having to pay five pounds. So I advised them to come on to Gloucester—well, they had to, of course: it's the first stop on the line—and told her my uncle would be at the station with my young cousin who was coming to school with me—I go to Branscombe Park, just out of Ludlow—and we'd ask him what they had best do. There should have been plenty of time, but unfortunately the train sat down just outside of Gloucester station—to think of its sins, I presume!—and we had just a minute or two for me to tell him what had happened. I had to leave them then, and he took them home with him, and did some odd spots of ringing up and so on. Then he took them to Swansea next day, where he had to go on business, anyhow, and one of your mistresses came to meet them and bring them here."

She paused, and looked at the interested faces turned up to her. "That is the true story of that episode," she said slowly, "and don't you believe anything else. It was nobody's fault, actually, for I suppose the porter was only trying to be helpful. It certainly wasn't *Peggy's* —or anyone else's of the party."

She finished, and was turning to Dickie, when a small voice rose painfully distinct. "I told you so, Phil Craven," it remarked. "It was just your nasty mind that made you think it was fishy!"

"Mary-Lou!" Dickie thundered. Nell hurriedly pulled

out her handkerchief and wiped her nose, long and thoroughly.

Mary-Lou stood up. "Please, Dickie," she said, "I'll apologize for dragging a—a private quarrel into public; but I was so glad *some*one could tell us the thing straight, I forgot."

"Very well: sit down now," Dickie said, rather helplessly; and Mary-Lou sat down with a complacent smile.

Nell spoke from behind her handkerchief. "I should think if that's a specimen of your juniors you could leave the rubbing-in part to them. I don't suppose any of your folk need say a thing more. Shall I go back to your room now to wait for Peggy while you dismiss the kids? O.K.," as Dickie nodded, "I'll just slip off, then."

She slipped off and found her way back to the prefects' room, where she was greeted five minutes later by an amazed Peggy, and Dickie left alone on the dais,, made a few pointed remarks about foolish gossip, and then dismissed her juniors to find their books for prep, which would begin in five minutes or so. The prefects left in a body, once Hall was cleared, quite satisfied that Nell was right, and that the younger girls could deal with the matter now. In point of fact, Blossom and Co. were so snubbed by those who had stood by Peggy, that they were thankful to let the whole thing drop, and a little extra vigilance on the part of the prefects soon put an end to any ideas anyone might have had about it's being 'all right' to be rude or impudent to prefects.

As for Eilunedd, the authoress of most of the trouble, she had *her* lesson on the Saturday from Jo herself, and it was as original as most of that lady's efforts were.

The Senior had been delighted with the invitation to "Come on to our place for tea after you've finished your shopping, won't you? We'll have tea for half-past three so that you can catch the five o'clock ferry. Come as soon as you can. What time shall I expect you?"

"We're going to shop in the morning, Mrs. Maynard," Eilunedd said. "We're having lunch in Carnbach, and if the Heads agree, I could be with you shortly after two.'.

183

"Oh, *good!*" Jo exclaimed. "I'll expect you about two, then."

Special Sixth had its shopping expedition, and lunched in a cafe, and all but Eilunedd caught the one o'clock ferry back to the island. Eilunedd, left alone, went for a walk along the sea-road; but, so afraid was she of being late, that she turned up at Cartref a good quarter of an hour early. Jo, knowing girls, had rather expected this, and was ready for her. She had arranged for lunch at half-past twelve, and then sent the boys out for a walk with Anna, so that she was quite free. When Eilunedd rang the doorbell, she appeared at the door, attired in an old coat covered with an apron.

"Hello!" she said. "Come along, Eilunedd. It's a lovely day—almost as mild as April, so I thought we'd go into the garden. You mayn't believe it, but we have some roses blooming, and I found two primroses out yesterday, as well as some of the winter pansies. I've two fowls to pluck for to-morrow's lunch. Robin and Daisy are both coming home to-night, and I expect Dr. Maynard as well, so I must be prepared. I thought I'd do them while we talked, and as it's such a mild day we'd be warm enough in the summer-house—through here, and across the lane, and in at the gate. Here's our garden! How do you like it?"

Eilunedd looked round the pretty garden where it felt quite warm, so sheltered was it, so soft the air to-day, and so bright the sun. Jo led the way to the summer-house at the far end, where old Rufus was stretched out in the sunshine, and pointed to a basket on the table.

"That's my little job just now—two plump chickens. Pull that chair out to the front and enjoy the sunlight, and tell me all the gossip while I start in." She sat down, unwrapped the white cloth over the basket, and lifted out the chickens. "I'll put the feathers back into the basket. Jack won't want to see his pretty garden strewn with feathers from end to end, and they are *awful* things for flying in every direction."

"Oh, but couldn't I help you?" Eilunedd asked eagerly.

Jo considered her gravely. "Ever feathered a chicken before?"

"No; but I'm sure I could if you showed me how. Please do! I'd like to try."

"O.K., if you feel like that about it. I took them on so that Anna could take the boys out. She can't do everything, and they had so much of the house during the stormy weather that I'm trying to get them into the open air as much as possible now, for I'm certain we shall have *weather* once the New Year comes. Look, Eilunedd; this is the way. Don't try to pull the other way or you'll tear the skin. They're young birds, so you'll find they feather fairly easily, I expect. Try not to let the feathers fly, or I shall hear about it from the doctor." She gave the girl a queer look as she saw her set to work, but Eilunedd, intent on this new occupation, never noticed it. Jo began on her own bird, and as her fingers flew she began talking about the early days of the school when it was in the Tirol.

Eilunedd listened, fascinated, even though she worked steadily. At first she was almost morbidly careful not to let her feathers fly. Then, as she became absorbed in Jo's tales, she grew careless. A tiny breeze was blowing, and first one or two, and then whole handfuls of feathers escaped, and went gaily across the garden. Finally, an especially large handful awoke Eilunedd to what she was doing, and she gave a cry of dismay.

"Oh, Mrs. Maynard! I'm so sorry! Never mind, though; I'll finish this, and then go and pick them up."

Jo had just finished her own bird. She took Eilunedd's from her. "If you really will try to collect them, I'll finish for you. You've done this jolly well for a first shot. Not a tear in the skin, and very evenly done. I'll soon finish now, and then we'll go and see about tea." Her fingers were flying as she spoke, and she looked up to give Eilunedd a nod of dismissal. That young lady hurried off to retrieve the feathers, and Jo, after working hard, finished the second chicken, popped the pair into her basket, and got up to go to the house.

"I'll go and see to tea while you finish," she called to her guest, who was climbing a rockery in quest of a tiny bunch of white feathers that had entangled themselves in the leaves of the winter saxifrage. "You come in when you've collected the feathers."

"Yes, thank you," Eilunedd panted, as she stretched out her hand.

Whish! came the wind; and the feathers floated serenely off towards the yellow winter jasmine that grew along one wall.

Jo went off, grinning broadly to herself. All the time she was filling the kettle and setting it on the gas, wheeling the tea-trolley, already laid with her pretty china and plates of wafer bread-and-butter and delicious home-made cakes, into the dining-room, she kept giving deep chuckles. Once she ran upstairs to a landing-window from which she could see the garden, and gazed out. The sight of her visitor laboriously picking up from the wide expanse of grass, while Rufus, who had remained with her, watched her gravely, following her from one place to another, caused her to collapse on to the stairs, and laugh till the tears came to her eyes. Then she heard the kettle boiling over, so she sprang to her feet, tore downstairs, and ten minutes later went to call Eilunedd. She found the girl very flushed and rather crestfallen. Feathers were still flying gaily about, and Eilunedd showed her a very small handful in a shamefaced way.

"These were all I could get, Mrs. Maynard. I'm awfully sorry to have been so careless. Shall I try again afterwards?"

Jo called Rufus, who came trotting up to her, and nuzzled his big head against her. "We'll go and have tea, Eilunedd, and talk about it while we're eating. It gets dark so soon now, I doubt if you could see. However, there's a fresh breeze now, so perhaps they will all have vanished by the morning," she added cheerfully.

Eilunedd followed her silently into the house. Jo showed her where to hang up her coat, and wash her hands, and when she was ready, took her into the drawing-room with its bright fire burning merrily, and tea waiting.

186

She settled her visitor in a chair, gave her tea and a hot scone, and then poured out her own cup.

"You know," she said conversationally, as she helped herself from the muffin-dish, "I often think *words* are like feathers."

Eilunedd looked at her. "How? I don't think I understand."

"Finish your scone and have another while they're hot. It's this way. You saw how the feathers flew every which way, and though I'm sure you worked hard, you couldn't get anything like even half of them when you set out to get them back? Well, it's the same sort of thing with things we say. Sometimes we say pleasant things— things that are helpful and kind, and those are the sort of words we don't want to recall. But sometimes we are angry, and we say unkind, bitter things. Later on, we may be sorry, and would give anything to unsay them; but that's something no one can do. And you never know just how much harm a thing like that may do someone else. It mayn't even be the person you meant it for. It may be someone quite different. Perhaps it's someone younger than yourself who gets wrong ideas from the things you've said. Perhaps you give hints of wrong ideas to those people, and they go on and make huge things of them, and it all causes awful trouble for everyone concerned." Jo paused to hold out her hand for Eilunedd's cup, but it wasn't given. The girl sat there, looking at her, a queer mixture of feelings struggling within her. She knew now that the invitation, the work on the birds and the feathers, had all been *meant*. She guessed that Jo knew a good deal more than she was saying, and she went hot as she suddenly thought of all she had done to make things uncomfortable for Peggy Bettany.

Jo saw it all. She reached forward and took the cup. "Was your tea as you liked it, Eilunedd? Enough cream in it?"

Eilunedd raised her shamed eyes, and saw that the subject was ended. Nothing more would be said here. But she also knew that Jo had said enough. Somehow she must try to undo the wrong she had done Peggy and help to bring the younger girls back to common sense. The trouble was that she had no idea how to manage it. She knew nothing, of course, about Nell Randolph and what had been said at the meeting the day before. She, in common with the rest of the Seniors, had taken it for granted that the younger girls had been treated to a sound lecture and perhaps threatened with a Head's report if they did not behave themselves better. That Nell had dissipated once for all the stupid story she had been largely instrumental in having broadcast was, as yet, unknown to her. Meantime, she must answer Jo's question about the tea. When that was over, Jo talked on easily about schooldays until it was time for the Senior to go to the ferry. Anna had brought the boys in by that time, and Jo took her to see them having their tea in the dining-room.

"What about our story, Mamma?" Stephen asked, when they had said "How do you do?" to the guest.

"Presently, Steve. I'm taking Eilunedd down to the ferry, and when I come back you can all come to the drawing-room and I'll tell you the story of how Thor tried out his strength against the giants. Finish your tea, and be washed and ready for me. I shan't be long. Come along, Eilunedd, or you'll miss the ferry and then I shall have to come over and make a worm of myself to Miss Annersley and Miss Wilson. Besides, aren't you in this *Little Women* business?"

Eilunedd nodded. "I'm *Hannah*," she said shyly.

"Then I'd have to face a raging Sixth as well, and that's more than even I like. So we'll make tracks, I think."

There was little time for chatter as they hurried through the blue winter twilight down to the ferry-landing, where they met a brisk wind. Jo laughed as she pulled her cap firmly down over her head.

"I don't think you need bother about those feathers, Eilunedd. This will clear them out of the garden all right. Here's the boat! You're just in nice time. Give my love to everyone, and say I wish I could have come

188

to see your show to-night; but with all the crowd coming home, I couldn't do it. I'll see you folk when you come over on Monday for rehearsal, and, of course, I'm coming, complete with family, on Tuesday. Then you folk depart on Thursday. What about the Hobbies show, by the way? Isn't that Wednesday afternoon? I'll pop over then—unless the weather goes bad on us again. Now you must go. Good night—and good luck!"

"Good night, Mrs. Maynard, and thank you—for everything!" Eilunedd got the words out awkwardly, and then ran. Jo turned after waving to her, and made her way home along the windy, lamp-lighted streets, laughing to herself now and then as she went. She was fairly sure that the girl had read her lesson right.

Miss Burn was at the ferry-landing on St. Briavel's to meet Eilunedd, and they hurried back to the Big House. In the entrance hall, they met Peggy as she came out of Hall, where she had been superintending final arrangements. Miss Burn left the two and raced upstairs to change for supper. Peggy just glanced at Eilunedd and was about to pass on, but the elder girl detained her.

"Wait a moment, please, Peggy. I—I want to speak to you."

Peggy stood still. She was by no means anxious to have any conversation with the girl who had tried to make things so unpleasant for her, but something in Eilunedd's eyes made her pause.

Eilunedd groped desperately for words. All the way over in the ferry she had been making up her mind to this. Now the moment was on her, she had no idea what to say.

"I—I——" she began.

The frostiness in Peggy's eyes melted a little. "Yes? What is it?" she asked gently.

"Oh—I'm sorry! I—I'd no right to talk to Blossom and the kids as I did. I—I wish I could unsay it, but I know I can't. But I'm sorry."

Peggy Bettany was a generous creature. She held out

her hand. "It's all right, Eilunedd. We'll say no more about it."

"That's all very well; but there are the kids. Since I talked, some of them have been playing up like demons. How are we going to stop that all at once?"

Peggy grinned suddenly. "Don't you worry about that. Nell Randolph, the niece of the man who looked after us, was over on yesterday's boat with her uncle and Dickie yanked her in to tell the whole story to the little dears. Nell was on the train, you see, and knew all about it— in fact, it was she that told me we would have to go to Gloucester. I'm told Mary-Lou and her tribe are rubbing it well into Blossom and Co. that they've made awful asses of themselves. You know what those imps can be like. I don't suppose there'll be much more trouble. Anyhow, term ends next week and they'll have the hols to come back to their senses. Now we'd better vamoose, or we'll be late for supper, and I've got to arrange my hair in ringlets before then, and it takes time to do that."

So that was all that was said, though Eilunedd did not forget Jo's lesson, and thereafter kept some sort of guard on her tongue.

'Little Women' went with a swing. Barbara was an excellent *Aunt March*, and tall Joan made a delightful *Laurie*, with Nita as *Jo* backing him up. Peggy, with her fair hair duly twisted into ringlets, each held in position by half a dozen hairpins, was an attractive *Amy*, though she complained later that she had never endured such tortures in her life, and at least half the hairpins were sticking straight into her scalp! Eilunedd, her mind freer than it had been all that term, gave the part of *Hannah* just the right amount of astringency; but the palm was borne off by Anthea Barnet as *Miss Crocker*, the nippy maiden lady who is one of the guests at *Jo's* unlucky luncheon party. How Anthea, who was normally a very pretty girl, managed to make herself look so unattractively middle-aged and unpleasant was a mystery to most people.

The Monday rehearsal was a fair one, though Mr. Denny wrung his hands when the choir suddenly went

flat during their rendering of 'What Child is This?' and
went on getting flatter and flatter, despite all Miss Cochrane's thumping out of the air in an attempt to pull them
up. In an 'action' carol, taken from an old Nativity
Play the school had given years ago when it was in Tirol,
Polly Winterton, who was playing the part of the Landlord
of the Inn, suddenly dried up, and stood going redder
and redder, while Bride Bettany, the St. Joseph, in an
effort to be helpful, dashed in half-way through the verse
that should have been sung in reply to her own, with an
indescribably funny effect. However, as Miss Wilson
said resignedly, they had had worse last rehearsals, so all
they could do was to hope for the best.

She proved to be justified next day when the Carol
Concert was an outstanding success—so much so, that
several of the audience were heard to say they would
have liked a second performance. However, that was
out of the question. When it was over, and the girls had
had a glorious tea-cum-supper, once the hall had cleared
they were hurried to the ferry, and the rest of the evening
was taken with packing up. Packing went on for some of
them next morning, while the rest prepared their Hobbies
show, to which only local friends could be invited, and
the few parents who had stayed on in Carnbach so as
to take their girls home with them on the Thursday.
Among these were Mrs. Bettany and Mrs. Winterton,
who were staying with Jo. Mrs. Winterton was stunned
with surprise when she saw Polly's pictures for the 'house',
as well as by the enormous improvement visible in her
pair of rebels. There was no doubt that they were happy,
and she really found it hard to believe that the prettily-
mannered girls who spoke so nicely, and treated her with
the same charming ways as the Bettany girls treated *their*
mother, could be the same two who had been threatened
with being sent to different schools and kept apart for a
whole year less than six months before.

Finally came Thursday and breaking-up. But news
from Canada arrived that morning for the school, and
after prayers, Miss Annersley read aloud to an enthralled

school an account of the christening of Kevin and Kester Russell which had come from 'Madame', as well as a letter of thanks for the christening present of silver napkin rings the school had sent for the Russell twins.

"And that's a really wizard top-off!" Lala Winterton remarked to Bride Bettany, as they set off for the ferry. "Well, I never thought I *should* like boarding-school of all things, but this has been an absolutely super three months!"

Polly, walking just in front with Maeve hanging on to her arm and Peggy at Maeve's other side, turned her head.

"Rather!" she agreed. "But hols are wizard too Peggy, some day when you crowd come to tea with us, we'll tell you about our special game, and if you like to join, we'll find parts for you."

"Parts?" Peggy queried, looking startled.

"Yes; I'm the Lady Acetylene Lampe, and Lala is her faithful attendant. We often used to play it, and I know you play just as mad things with your kids. Perhaps we're getting a bit old for pretence games now, but just for once I'd like to do it with a few more of us—more fun!"

"Oh!" screamed Maeve excitedly, "Maurice and me'll be your children, and we'll have a kidnapping!"

"We never tried that. It's a jolly good idea. Somehow, though, it may be the last time we'll want to do it. I rather think it'll be a really super scheme," the Lady Acetylene Lampe replied, as they began to run to catch up with the others who had gone ahead.

It was!